A Hole in Time

Clark Graham

Cover art by JJ Schutza

elvenshore.blogspot.com

elvenshore@gmail.com

A Hole in Time

© Clark Graham 2016

All Rights Reserved

The Time Loop Series

Book One

A Loop in Time

Book Two

A Hole in Time

Book Three?

(None Yet)

A Hole in Time

    Chapter One

    Chapter Two

    Chapter Three

    Chapter Four

    Chapter Five

    Chapter Six

    Chapter Seven

    Chapter Eight

    Chapter Nine

    Chapter Ten

    Chapter Eleven

    Chapter Tewelve

    Chapter Thirteen

    Chapter Fourteen

    Chapter Fifteen

    Chapter Sixteen

    Chapter Seventeen

    Chapter Eighteen

    Chapter Nineteen

    Chapter Twenty

    Chapter Twenty-One

    Chapter Twenty-Two

Chapter Twenty-Three

Chapter Twenty-Four

Chapter Twenty-Five

Chapter Twenty-Six

Chapter Twenty-Seven

Chapter Twenty-Eight

Chapter Twenty-Nine

Chapter Thirty

Chapter Thirty-One

Chapter Thirty-Two

Chapter Thirty-Three

Chapter Thirty-Four

Chapter Thirty-Five

Chapter Thirty-Six

Chapter Thirty-Seven

Chapter Thirty-Eight

Chapter Thirty-Nine

Chapter Forty

Chapter Forty-One

Chapter Forty-Two

Chapter Forty-Three

Chapter Forty-Four

Chapter Forty-Five

Chapter Forty-Six

Chapter Forty-Seven

Chapter Forty-Eight

Chapter Forty-Nine

Chapter Fifty

Sample Chapter

Chapter 1: Montana

Chapter One

"A time machine!" Colonel Russell Roberts spewed his mouthful of coffee all over his olive drab desk. The balding man had been relegated to a Washington paper-pushing job. It was his pre-retirement position. He had been all over the world for his country in the army. This is how they thanked him. Roberts did the twenty-five year mandatory review of top secret files to see if they met the nine narrow exceptions that allowed them to remain classified beyond that point.

The job was mundane. Technology items that had gone through the whole twenty-five years of classification were usually already available in the private sector. The review was just a formality. It wasn't until he reached the file marked *Vmax3 Drive Project* that he sat up and took notice. As he read the file, the hairs on the back of his neck stood up. He couldn't believe what he was reading. This was huge. How could it have been buried for so long? He phoned his superior.

"General, I have a file that needs an exception. You're going to want to see this, Sir."

The file bounced its way up the chain of command, eventually reaching the desk of Lieutenant General Aston Williams. He was an ambitious man who had worked his way up the military brass by being a risk taker, and an innovator. If someone were to get things done, in a peace time army, it'd be him. He had the political backing and a lot of hidden funds enabling him to complete projects no one else could touch.

The tall, lean General had just a smattering of gray on the sides of his dark, full head of hair. He carried himself straight and upright. 'No' was a word he didn't tolerate. His aide, Major Robert Dalton waited for the general as he entered.

"Sir, good morning, Sir. The file on your desk is the one causing all the fuss."

"The time machine file,." Williams snickered. "Have you reviewed it? Is it just a bunch of hocus pocus?"
The Major was worried. A person didn't waste the Generals time or they wouldn't be his aide for long. Before Dalton, Williams had gone through twenty-tree aides in one year. Dalton was now in his third year in this position. He had close cropped hair. He thought having blonde hair, a gift from his German mother, might be a stigma in the army. The perception of being slow witted, whether real or imagined, could be a career killer. So he kept it short and under a cap at all times.

"It looks pretty legit, Sir."

"How did a time machine not get the attention of several levels at the Pentagon?"

"The Vamx3 Project was thought to be a complete failure. The plane disappeared without a trace and the project was scrapped. What wasn't in the official report, but is in the file, was the fact that the pilot showed up the next day, forty five years older. The only reason we're finding out about all of this now is that the information had been boxed up and stuck on the back shelf of the archives. It's come due for its twenty five year review. Instead of the incomplete report, issued at the time, it has the whole story of the incident."

The general sat down and picked up the report.

Knowing it would take Williams several hours to go through it, Dalton busied himself with his regular duties. It wasn't until he called the general at lunch time that he found out how it was going.

"Sir, can I bring you something to eat?"

"Not now," the general barked.

When Williams was working on a project, he always skipped lunch.

Two hours later, General Williams emerged from his office. "I need you to organize a committee to study this file. I need two computer modeling gurus and three mechanical engineers, along with a history buff and some type of shrink. All of them have to have top secret clearance. I want to see where to go from here. I'm not totally onboard with the time travel thing, but it's too important to ignore."

"Yes, Sir." As Williams started to go back into his office, the major asked, "What shall we call this project, Sir?"

Williams turned back. "Call it Project Black Hole, because that's where our careers will be going if we develop this and it fails."

The major swallowed involuntarily. "Yes, Sir."

Dalton knew just who to call. Major Dempsey and Captain Acker were the best computer modelers in the army. Lieutenant Salazar, Major Carlson, and Captain Tegan had worked with Williams on the last project. Colonel Ross was the best in the business when it came to history. The psychologist threw him. He didn't understand why they needed one in the first place, so finding one that would do exactly what the general wanted was going to be problematic. One didn't question Williams; they just did what he ordered. Finally, the major decided on Major Zunino, mainly because he liked his name.

Chapter Two

Project Black Hole. It sounded ominous, the forty year old Major Dempsey thought. As he looked around the room, he saw the quality of the men they brought onboard. It had to be something big for General Williams to round up this group. He had never seen the man on the end. The name on the uniform said Zunino. He was weird looking. He had longer hair than the services usually allowed. His teeth were pushed out in the middle, forming a shallow V-shape. His eyes were deep set and his hair was jet black.

The others in the room, Dempsey had worked with before. He and Ackers had been on so many of these projects together, they could usually tell what the other was thinking, without saying anything. The engineers on the other side of the table he knew well. Seeing these men all in one place was unusual. Normally only one of them, in a rare instance, two, would be assigned to a particular project. Having three of them meant something big was up.

Dempsey considered himself a Civil War buff, but not to the degree of Colonel Ross. They could spend hours just talking about the war alone. Ross was a large, round man, more at home reading books than he was at the gym. Many of his commanders had threatened to drum him out of the army for his weight, but in the end, he was always that invaluable asset they could never get rid of.

Sitting around the conference table, they were waiting for the meeting to start. It was the typical room, set up the way General Williams always insisted upon. Two bookshelves at the end of the room held the information they would need for research. Computers along both of the side walls.

The screens always faced inward so the general could sit at the head of the table and see at a glance what everyone was working on.

Williams had a well-earned reputation as a control freak. He was hard to work for, but the man got results.

Major Dalton came into the room and handed out folders. Dempsey opened his right away to see what was happening. The file labeled Vmax3 drive made him scratch his head. It didn't sound important. A minute later, the general himself entered. The men all stood and saluted.

"At ease, gentlemen." Williams waited for the men to be seated. "What you have in front of you is a schematic of the Vmax3 drive. I want to make a computer model of the drive and see what it actually does and doesn't do."

"Begging your pardon, Sir," Colonel Ross said. "The Vmax3 has been tested. Way back in 2014, it was found to be faulty, causing the loss of the pilot. The project was scrapped."

The general smiled. "Colonel, you do know your history. It looks like Major Dalton chose the right man for the job. However, the official report doesn't tell the whole truth. The pilot didn't die. He showed up the next morning, very much alive. The only difference is, he had aged forty-five years in one day."

Dalton was on the edge of his seat, waiting for this moment. He had wondered how the general was going to break the news and Ross' comment couldn't have come at a better time. The room fell into a stunned silence.

"Gentlemen, what we may have discovered back in the archives, hidden on a shelf, is a time machine." The general had his arms behind his back as he talked. He only did this when he was in complete control of a situation. "It is your job to prove or disprove that. This is of the utmost secrecy. No one outside this room, not even the President of the United States, is allowed to know what we are working on here." He cleared his throat. "Major Dempsey and Captain Acker, you will take the data the engineers give you and make a computer model of it. Colonel Ross, you will find out everything about the people that worked on the original Vmax3 Drive and give that information to Major Zunino. Major, your job is to tell us why these men hid this report for the past twenty five years. I want reasons, and the thought processes, for every decision they made. Any questions?"

Everyone shook their heads. No one had enough to go on to even ask a question. Turning, the general left the room. When Dalton stood up to follow, Major Dempsey asked, "Is my calendar wrong? This isn't April first, is it?"

"No, this isn't April fools day, but you may have just entered the twilight zone. Only time will tell." Dalton smiled, then headed through the door.

Chapter Three

Four weeks into the project, the computer model was in the early stages. Pages and pages of documents had been gone through with the engineers. Major Dempsey was running a preliminary test on the system. The plane and the drive matrix had been input, along with all of the data from the first test flight. The problem was, it didn't work.

The plane would create a vortex behind it and then disintegrate, over and over again.

The general visited the room to check on the progress two or three times a day. At other times, it was left to Major Dalton to inform him of any breakthroughs. With everything that was going on, Dalton decided it was time to call a meeting so everyone could report on the findings.

The general strode into the room. "What have we found out? Major Dempsey, we will start with you."

Dempsey walked over to the computer and ran the simulation. "We haven't completed the model, but we have found one flaw in the original design. The F117 fighter is not the right airframe for this engine. We have an unknown vortex that causes catastrophic failure in every model we have run so far." He showed the computer model to the group. The fighter was just lines, like a stick figure, but it was easy to see when it fell apart.

"Can you analyze what the vortex is?"

"Not until we finish."

"Is there any indication of time travel in what you have?"

"There are so many unknowns, it's hard to say what happens right before the plane flies apart. If this time machine is going to become a reality, it's going to need a brand new airframe that can handle the forces put upon it."

"Very good. What have you found out, Colonel Ross?"

"Sir, I have followed the lives of John Buck and Jason Ralston, along with every officer who were in the room when the files were sealed. First, let's look at John Buck. He appeared in an army hospital in 1966. He had no prior records. There is no birth record for him or any information of where he went to school or anything. He just appeared, as if out of thin air. After being diagnosed with amnesia, he was released. From there, he found work in a hardware store and then he obtained his pilot's license in record time. He worked as a crop duster in Idaho for a few years. He would have been in his twenties when we have the first records of him. He married Bobby Sue Phillips for one day then had it annulled. She married a Dr. Tim Ralston a short time after that."

Ross stood up and made his way to the white board at the front of the room. "Two things are significant here." He wrote *Bobby Sue Phillips* and *Dr. Tim Ralston* on the board. The he drew a line under each of them and wrote *Steve Ralston.* "These two had a son named Steve." Then he drew a line under Steve's name and wrote Jason Ralston. "If John Buck was Jason Ralston, then he married his grandmother. "What exactly does that mean?" The general's brow furrowed and his arms folded.

"It could mean he was his own grandfather, but we have no way of proving that. It's also interesting that after he married a second time, he stopped crop dusting and lived on his investments. He never once lost money on a stock and he knew exactly when to buy and when to sell. He was either a financial genius or he had come from the future, into the past."

"So you think this time travel actually happened?"

"I still have my doubts, but not as many as I started out with. When Jason Ralston's father died in a car accident, it was John Buck who supported Jason's family financially, including the buying of a house. There is a connection there. I also looked at the lab's DNA results. The tests were either faked or John Buck and Jason Ralston, were in fact, one in the same person."

Major Dempsey watched the general's reaction. He looked like a statue, unmoved, but his eyes gave him away. He was shocked at what he was hearing.

Clearing his throat, Williams turned to Zunino. "What do you have major?"

"As you probably know, it's not easy to figure out the state of mind of a person, especially when the decisions they made were twenty-five years ago. I learned that two of the participants were still alive, so I asked permission to interview them on the pretense of a data collection about the Vmax3 project. Captains Jacobs and Smith are both retired Air Force. Jacobs refused to talk to me, but Captain Smith agreed to a meeting. It was going well, but when I mentioned the name John Buck, he stood up and said the meeting was over. I can only believe it was their deep secret, even after all these years. Even though there are only a few of the men left who were there, they don't want any information about the project to get out there."

"Okay, thank you, gentlemen. We will continue to work on this project until we have explored all possibilities."

Dempsey knew the meeting was over, but he watched the men file out. He went back to his computer. It was the perfect job for an introvert like himself. He stayed two hours after quitting time. His wife called his computer, his mistress. He would spend more time with it than her.

Chapter Four

Three weeks later, the work accomplished, the final reports in, the men waited for what would happen next. It wasn't a surprise to see Williams enter the room with Senator James. James held the purse strings for the government. This project would go no further without him putting his John Hancock on the bottom line.

Lean and with a full head of light brown hair, James was all business. The hair, like the senator, wasn't genuine. The implants, without which James would be completely bald, were obvious. Dalton knew the senator had convinced himself the only way to get elected was to have a full head of hair, so he went out and got one.

The man held the keys to a lot of research money and was Williams's go-to guy for funding.

"Good morning, men. We are ready to hear your reports."

"Yes, Sir," Major Dempsey stood up. "If you will please turn towards the screen, I'll run you through the computer model." "Here we have the original F117A flying with the Vmax3 engine. When the engine was turned on, the plane hyper-accelerated to Mach 2.5. The vortex formed, putting even more stress on the overburdened airframe and it flew apart. It was a miracle anyone made it out alive."

Starting the model over, Dempsey slowed it down. "Now if we take the same model and play it five times slower, we can see the vortex form around the plane. Using the information from the original files of the test flight, we can see the timeline going backwards when the vortex forms. It stops in 1966. It is the creation of the vortex that causes the timeline change. It's like drilling a hole in time."

The senator's jaw dropped open, his eyes were big and round.

"So according to this model, Jason Ralston did go back in time forty-five years?" The general ignored the stunned senator.

"Yes, Sir. It's all making sense now that we added a time line to the model and understand the forces at work."

"Is this time travel practical, or are we going to send pilots all over the timeline and not be able to bring them home?"

Dalton watched the senator. He looked pale and clammy, as if he might have a heart attack at any moment.

"Sir," Dempsey continued, "We have created a second model using the information the engineers gave us. If we were going to make a time machine, it would have to have a much sturdier airframe specifically designed for the stresses the vortex will put on it. Having done this in the next simulation, we're able to go back in time, a year, a hundred years, or even a thousand years using this technology. We can accurately arrive there on the very day we need to. It's just a matter of getting the plane airborne so the engine can create the vortex."

"Fascinating, and how about coming back home?"

"It is the simple process of reversing the spin on the Vmax3 engine. When that's done, according to the computer model, the machine will go forward in time."

"What do you have to report, Colonel Ross?" The general managed a smile. He was in his glory with the possibility of his greatest achievement yet.

"According to all the records that John Buck left, he stated that time was a loop. Once in the loop, everything progresses the same every time. So if we are able to go back in time, it would mean that we have already been there before. Like John did."

"So you think we will not be able to change the timeline?" The smile was gone.

"Not according to the only man that ever time traveled."

Major Zunino raised his hand.

"Yes, Major."

"Sir, I can address that. John Buck went back in time, that is true, and everything turned out exactly the same, time after time. However, he was in the same circumstance with the same people and he made the same decisions each time. John made an effort not to disturb the time line. He looped because he wanted to loop. If he had made a different decision each time, it is probable the time line would have changed. In fact, I don't see a way it could have stayed the same."

"Very good job, gentlemen. Take a few days off. You will be notified if we will get the funding to continue the Black Hole Project, or if you're to be reassigned."

The men filed out, except for Dalton, Williams, and Senator James.

When the door closed, James stood up. "Are you people mad? A time machine? You have lost your mind."

Dalton had expected this reaction. James was always the dramatic type. "If you please, Sir, here is a copy of all the files regarding this project. They have to stay in this room, but read them over and then tell us what you think."

James looked at Dalton and then at Williams. Shaking his head, he sat down and opened the file.

Chapter Five

A week later, the group, minus Major Zunino, sat around the same table again. When the general and Major Dalton entered the room, the general was all smiles. Major Dempsey knew this meant he was able to get the funding.

"Gentlemen, it's a go. Our only requirement comes from Senator James. He wants our first mission to be the erasing of Adolf Hitler from the history books. I can't wait to see how much of a better place the world will be after we go back and fix things, so to speak."

Dempsey wasn't so sure. They could fix one thing and destroy another. Who knows how bad the time line would be messed up after they fixed it?

When the general left the room, Dempsey went over to Dalton. "How did he get the money and how much did he get? Projects like this run into the billions, especially with the development of a new plane."

"He only has a couple hundred million. That's how he always does it. Then when he spends that, he tells them he needs a little more, and if he stops now, they will have wasted all that money they already spent. After doing it three or four times, he'll have enough to finish the project."

"I see. Where did Major Zunino go?"

"He's been reassigned. As we go into the development phase, we will need more engineers and less modelers, too."

"I want to see how this ends. Can you put in the good word for me?"

Dalton smiled, "Yes, I can do that. We'll need a couple of good pilots. Can you recommend anyone?"

"Besides you, of course, I have a buddy in 307th. I can ask him for a recommendation."

"They will have to be fluent in German."

Dempsey hadn't realized that. "Of course they would. You guys think of everything."

"We try." Dalton went to go and check on the other men.

Dempsey sat down at his computer. One of the engineers had given him a new set of parameters to model so he started working on it.

A week later, there was another meeting. When Dempsey arrived, he saw empty chairs where the other modelers had been. Three new engineers followed General Williams into the room. Dalton handed out folders.

The general cleared his throat. "Gentlemen, we have now entered the design phase of this project. In front of you are the specifications we have created during the modeling phase. In a nutshell, we have a beefed-up airframe able to withstand the pressures the Vmax3 drive will put on it. In addition, the plane will have a storage area for the change of clothes and gear that will be required. A tandem seating arrangement for the two pilots and the Vmax3 drive will sit over the regular jet engine. It has to have total VTOL capabilities, so the pilots can land the plane in the woods without a runway for takeoff and landing. It's going to be an ugly duckling, but very functional for our needs.

"I have with me, Major Ellis, Major Larson, and Captain Watson. They are joining the team. We've also lost a few people along the way, but this team will stick together to see the project to its completion. Thank you, gentlemen, and let's get to work."

Dempsey went back to his computer, inputting the latest data from the engineers. He was working a lot of overtime at this point. As the criteria for the new plane began to take shape, the designs were changing on an almost daily basis. The computer models showed that the wings were too weak, so they beefed them up, which made the plane bigger. The Vmax3 drive, when put in regular mode, worked fine, but when they reversed the drive to go forward in time, it caused more stress. The engineers had to add a lot more structure to the plane to prevent it from coming apart. Every change seemed to make the plane larger and more expensive. As the estimated costs of the plane went up, the morale of the group went down. Everyone expected to run out of money and have to scrap the project.

The general's mood was souring, too. Dempsey hated it when he visited. He would look at the progress and see what a monstrosity the plane was becoming, then shake his head. Time and time again, the general would sit down and mumble something about needing a drink. Finally, after a year and a half, the design phase was over. The whole group was on stand down until more funding could be acquired and the plans could be sent out to manufacturers for bids. The general was so tense, everyone just stayed out of his way.

Dalton came up to Dempsey one day. "You're now part of the inner circle. You've been invited to the general's home for dinner and drinks."

Dempsey was surprised. "Thanks, what time?"

"I have it all written down, along with directions. See you there?"

"Yes, of course."

Dempsey had always been a computer geek through his high school and college experience. He knew the general had his favorites, but now he was one of them. Now he would be part of the inner circle. He was ecstatic.

Chapter Six

Saturday night came around and Dempsey, along with his wife, Lisa, drove out to the Hamptons. The major had never been there before, preferring the Carolina coast for any and all of his vacations. He and Lisa had been married twenty years and raised a daughter, who was now away at college. When they drove up to the address Dalton had given them, he was surprised to see a large, Victorian era, house. It had stone walls and was two stories high.

"Wow, this is really nice," Lisa said as they got out of the car. They knocked on the door and were let in by the general's wife, Caroline. She was blonde and tall compared to Lisa, who was just over five three with jet black hair.

Caroline led them into the living room where the group was gathered. Major Dalton, along with Colonel Ross sat down on the coach. The doorways were arched and the ceiling vaulted. Wrought iron lamps lit the room, showcasing the antique furniture.

"Oh, good, you found the place, welcome," the general said.

"I keep telling my husband he needs to become a general so he can afford a place like this," Lisa replied.

Williams laughed. "It's all sweat equity, I'm afraid. No need to be impressed. I bought this place for pennies on the dollar. It was mostly blown down by the last hurricane. What did survive was damaged in a fire a few years later. Some kids were having a party in here and their bonfire got carried away. I've been restoring it as I go. After dinner I'll take you on a tour, if you wish."

"That would be lovely," Lisa replied.

Knowing that discussing the Black Hole Project was taboo in front of the others, the group talked about history. "Did you know that this area was farmland up until the 1890s? Then it became a popular place for New York's well-heeled to come for their vacations. Actually, I've done some research on this very house. It was built by a man named Dalton, an investor who struck it rich. He could be a relative of yours, Major."

"No, none of my relatives have ever been rich," Major Dalton replied.

"J. Adalwolf Dalton was the man's name." Ross went on. He didn't notice the major's eyes widened while Ross talked.

"I have some appetizers." Caroline stood up, obviously not a fan of history. "Honey, will you help me bring out the trays?" It was more a command than a question.

"I'm never the general in my own home." Williams sighed. He followed his wife into the kitchen.

"Even if he did rebuild it himself, it still would have cost a pretty penny," Lisa said.

"The general's family has old money. They have lived on Long Island for a long time. His father has a home out here, also. It's right on the water," Ross replied.

The general and Caroline came back in carrying two trays of hors d'oeuvres and set them down on the coffee table. "Don't be shy." Caroline picked one up. "Dig in." The others followed suit.

They made small talk until the caterers came an hour later. Moving into the dining room, the large table had room enough for all of them. It had a crystal chandelier in the middle.

"That's one of the only nice things that survived," the general commented when he noticed Lisa eyeing it.

"It's beautiful."

The group enjoyed their dinner of roasted stuffed game hens with wild rice and salad. After dinner, they made their way back into the living room.

"At this point of the evening, we should be sitting around a fire enjoying our drinks, but the fireplace hasn't been restored yet, so we'll just have to do in here." The general sipped his bourbon.

After a couple of drinks, the general took them on a tour of the house. "Only the dining room, living room, bedroom, and kitchen are complete, and of course, the bathroom. Not having to use the outhouse in the winter is a blessing."

"He's just kidding," Caroline added.

"We decided that those rooms had to be the minimum requirement for us to move out here. I've been too busy lately to take time off, but things should settle down soon and we'll finish the den and the other bedrooms."

He opened the door to the unfinished part of the house. Dempsey could see the burnt timbers and taped up windows.

"This is the den. The chimney blew down in the hurricane. What was left was plugged up with debris. When the kids lit the fire, it damaged this part of the house."

"I thought the hurricane did more damage than just blow out some windows." Lisa said.

"It took out all of the out buildings and the storm surge caused flooding. All of the plaster will have to be taken out in this part of the building, like it was in the other parts. That's next year's chore."

"Oh, okay."

A few hours later, Major Dempsey and Lisa headed back home. She looked around at all the mansions. "Would you want to live like this, Honey?"

"No, just give me a simple life. I'm okay with that."

"I think I could get used to this."

The Major didn't know how what to say so he kept quiet. He felt she would always want more than they had.

Ross and Dalton had driven in together. When they were in the car on the way back to their homes, Dalton turned to Ross. "Not right now, because I know you're busy, but someday, I want you to find out if I'm related to this R. Adalwolf Dalton who built the house."

Ross' brow furrowed. "I thought you said you didn't come from money."

"I don't, but still, there are similarities I find interesting, I'm just curious. Do you know what the initial R stood for?"

"I don't know. The man never used his first name, just the initial, but after this project is over, I'll research it for you."

"Thanks."

Chapter Seven

Major Dempsey arrived at work early Monday morning and he was finishing up the last computer model. All of the design specs were in, and this time, everything was working as it should. He went over and over the program, trying everything to break the plane, but the thing was built like a fort at this point. Even full application of the Vmax3 drive from full forward to full reverse didn't destroy it.

Being so involved in the modeling, Dempsey didn't hear the general come in the room. "So, how's it looking?"

The major nearly came out of his skin. "Sir, I didn't see you, Sir." He looked at his watch and then looked around the room, "Where is everyone?"

"Home, I imagine. I was able to get a hold of them before they came in. We're relocating to Seattle. We have the go ahead for the next phase." The general's face lit up in a big smile.

"Seattle? When do we start?" The major hadn't thought about the implications of actually succeeding. He was both excited about the project going forward and dreading the move. It would mean time away from the family. His wife never followed him on temporary assignments.

"We should be moved in two weeks. Boeing was the winning bidder and we'll develop the plane in one of their hangars."

"Yes, Sir."

"Go home and start packing your bags. When you get to Seattle, all of the computers and data will be out there."

"What about you, Sir. How will you finish restoring your house?"

"There will be plenty of time for that when we finish this project."

"Yes, Sir."

The general left. Dempsey ran the simulation one more time, then he turned off his computer and headed home. His wife would be surprised to see him in the middle of the day, but he dreaded the part where he would have to tell her he was going away again. Trying to get her out of that house was impossible. She wasn't going to leave her home for any extended period.

Dalton received the news when he was still at home. He'd hoped the plane would be built at the Skunk Works so he could enjoy the California sunshine. Instead he would have to endure the endless Seattle rain. With a big sigh, he started arranging everyone's flights and the moving of the equipment.

At the party, he's seen the colonel's and the major's wives. They seemed happy. He had made a conscious choice not to marry, as his career was his main focus, now he second guessed that decision. Having a wife didn't seem to slow down the careers of those around him. He sighed and went back to the relocation of the project. Curing his loneliness would have to wait. The project comes first.

He finished the task hours later and headed back to his apartment. He had saved so much money over the years by not buying a house. What did he need, but a stove, bed, and easy chair? He was rethinking that decision after visiting the general and seeing how much more comfortable he was.

Colonel Ross decided to drive across the country to Seattle, instead of flying with the rest of them. He was getting older and had always wanted to do the trip. This move was the perfect excuse. The colonel had been all alone since his wife died three years ago. His three kids were spread out all over the United States. He would visit all of them during the trip, knowing he would get fussed at by his daughter for his weight, but he deserved it. Gaining was always a whole lot easier than losing. He sat down and opened up the photo album, as he did every time there was a life change. Tears graced his cheeks as he saw the love of his life playing with the kids. She'd left a hole when she died.

Photo albums were such a thing of the past in the modern digital world. New ones were hard to find. He loved his. He would curl up in his easy chair and flip through the photos, get lost in his memories, cry a little bit, then flip the next page. It was all he had left.

Chapter Eight

It was raining when Major Dalton's plane touched down in Seattle. He was the last of the team to arrive because he had to make some last minute arrangements to get the rest of the equipment shipped out. He hurried to the hanger that would be the base of operations for this part of the project. There were two Air Force guards in front of the conference room General Williams had set up for his headquarters. It was the same arrangement that they had in Washington, only the room was larger. Dalton flashed his ID to get past them. When inside he saw all the familiar faces. Dempsey turned from his computer. "Have you met the project manager yet?"

"No, I just now got in."

"Come on, I'll introduce you." Dempsey led him out of the conference room and into an office three doors down.

Philip Anderson sat behind a computer, standing as soon as the two men entered the room. The blond, blue-eyed Swede stood a good six four, thin and muscular. "Hello."

"Phil, this is Major Dalton. He's the assistant of General Williams."

"It's good to meet you, Major. Your general is occupying the office next to mine. I leave my door open so if you need to talk to me, come on in. Well, as long as there is no one else in the room."

"Good to meet you, too, Phil."

"It's a good project to work on, but I'm hearing that there are some things you can't discuss with me or my men, even though we all have security clearances."

"Yes, well, it's a highly experimental bird. It may or it may not work, so until we find out everything this thing does, we are keeping it under wraps."

"Very well. If there is anything I can do to assist you, let me know."

"Thank you so much."

The two majors left the room, Dempsey smiled. "He's dying to find out what's so special about this plane. He keeps probing, but he's getting nowhere. To him it's only an overpriced, overweight bird with an extra engine that's mostly useless."

"I'm sure the general wants him left out of the loop. Telling the senator was bad enough, but necessary to get the funding."

"Of course."

They both flashed their badges as they passed back through the security guards. Dempsey picked up a stack of papers the engineers had left in his box before turning to Dalton. "I'm sure it's eating Phil alive that we've posted guards on this room. They normally have complete access to Air Force projects."

"I'm sure it is. Is the general in yet?"

"He was the first to arrive. He's sitting in his office. Oh, by the way, he has strict orders that no information about what the project does is to leave this room. If you need to show him something, he directed us to come and get him and bring him here."

"Thanks for the heads up."

When the general found out that Dalton had arrived, he came into the conference room to talk to him. "Have a good flight?"

"Yes, Sir."

"I will show you to your quarters. We've rented some condos for the group. It's not far from here. Where are your bags?"

"I left them in the rental car."

The two men drove over to the condominiums. When Dalton walked into his, he looked around. The colors were drab, pastels mostly. Beige and brown trim weren't Dalton's thing, but it was what the general liked, so he said, "It's nice."

"These Boeing guys are going crazy, trying to figure out what we're doing. I had to have the room checked for bugs, there weren't any. Still, I don't trust them."

"They all have security clearances, but even so, the project manager, Phil, did try to get information out of me. I just think that they are usually in the know and not being on this project is driving them crazy."

The general smiled, "I guess, but I still don't want them to know."

"Of course not. Maybe we could make up something?"

"No, they would see right through that. Best to keep them guessing."

Dalton unpacked. He traveled light, so there wasn't a lot to do. When he was done he asked, "Should we get back?"

"No, you just got in. I think we'll grab something to eat and then take the rest of the day off. They can do without us for the next few hours."

"Yes, Sir."

They both changed out of their uniforms and into civilian clothes and went out on the town, stopping for drinks at a waterfront lounge. It was late when they arrived back so Dalton went straight to bed. The general, whose condo was next door to Dalton's, called home before retiring for the night. Caroline was a night owl. Even with the time zone difference, she'd be awake.

Chapter Nine

Scratching his head, Phillip Anderson looked over the blueprints the Air Force had giving him. It didn't make any sense. He had no idea what this machine was supposed to do. Obviously, the Vmax3 drive was the star of the show. Having worked for Boeing for twenty-one years, he thought he'd seen every type of engine, but this one was completely different. He walked over to the door of the conference room. He called ahead as the guards would never let him through.

"What can I do for you, Phil?"

"I'm just outside. Do you have time to come out and talk?"

"Sure, I'll be right out." Dalton came through the door in under a minute. There was another conference room next door to the one the Air Force occupied. They used it for joint meetings between the groups. Phil motioned to the door and Dalton followed him in.

Laying the plans for the Vmax3 drive on the table, Phil started in, "This has decades-old technology in it. Can we at least upgrade to more modern standards?"

"No, the drive has to be built exactly per specifications. If anything is even slightly off, the drive might not function as it was intended."

Phil smiled to himself. *That was it.* It was all about this Vmax3 drive. His friends with the big pocket books, as he called them, would be very interested. "Okay, we'll build it exactly as it was designed."

"Is there anything else?"

"No, that will do."

The Major didn't go back to the conference room, but straight into the general's office.

He knocked on the door. The general beckoned him in. The back wall of the office was glass and overlooked the hanger where the plane was being built. "Isn't much to look at yet, but some of it is coming along."

There was just the skeleton frame of the airplane, rivets and green primer fuselage parts bolted together.

"Yes, Sir."

Williams turned back around to face the major. "What can I do for you?"

"Sir, Philip Anderson is probing again. Can we get him off this project and get someone we trust?"

The general smiled. "Boeing said they had a leak, but couldn't find out who it was. When we complained about Anderson, they started investigating him. Turns out he has accounts in the Cayman Islands, worth a lot of money. He'll be going to jail soon."

"Oh no, he has the plans for the Vmax3 drive. We have to get those from him." Dalton's heart raced. He turned to go get the plans back.

"No, he doesn't. He has plans for a factious drive. That's the thing they will hang him on. The real Vmax3 drive is being built in the Skunk Works in California. I thought it would be better if we didn't put all of our eggs in one basket. They don't know what the plane will look like and these guys won't know what the drive looks like until they put it in the plane."

Dalton calmed down. "Yes, Sir, very good, Sir."

The general grabbed Major Dalton's personnel file from the stack of papers on the desk.

"You've been holding out on me."

"Sir, I don't understand, Sir." Dalton swallowed hard.

Williams picked up the file and paraphrased it. "Your mother's name was Felicia Schmidt. She married your father while he was stationed in Germany. You grew up and went to public school until it was time for college, deciding to go to the Air Force Academy, instead of staying in Germany. Your father was a well-connected major by that point, so it was easy for you to get in. While you were there, you showed exceptional skill in flying and graduated nearly at the top of your class."

"Yes, Sir, but you've read all of this before."

"I didn't need a German-speaking pilot before this. I'd hate to lose you as an assistant, but I need you more for this mission, than I do as an assistant."

"Yes, Sir." Dalton wanted to say no, but he knew that if he did, the general would ruin the rest of his career. He never had any other choice. He felt doomed either way.

"You have been the best assistant I've ever had, but you're perfect for this mission. I need someone I have total trust in. You're going to be flying that plane."

"Thank you, Sir."

"I have a Captain Gerald Myers, who also speaks fluent German, and is an excellent pilot. He will be joining you on these missions. There's a promotion in the works for you, also. The paperwork is going through the channels as we speak. When all of this is said and done, you'll be a colonel and in charge of this project."

"Yes, Sir."

The general added. "You have a chance to rewrite history, over and over again. That should be a huge honor."

"Of course, Sir, it is, Sir."

The general turned back to the project list and Dalton left the office. He made his way back into the conference room they used as the project command center. He flashed his badge to the guards. He sat down in a quiet corner and pretended to be working. He wondered why the general had ignored the part in the report where his fighter jet had both engines cut out and he had to eject, breaking his legs when he landed. He had vowed he would never fly again.

Chapter Ten

After locking the door to his office, he took out his phone his 'friends' gave him, Phil scanned in the plans for the Vmax3 drive. When working in the Phantom Works, no one was allowed to a personal phone, only the one issued by the company. This phone was identical to the one Boeing had issued him, except for the fact that it had a scanner built in. At a glance it was no different and it would have to be taken apart before anyone figured out it wasn't the same phone.

Phil confidently put the phone in his pocket and then headed towards the gate to go for lunch. When he drove up, to his surprise the guard asked him to step out of the car.

"What is the meaning of this? I'm a busy man. I'll have your job, now open the gate. I have a lunch appointment."

"Please, Sir, step out of the car."

"You're an idiot." Phil slammed his car into reverse, but before he could move, two security cars pulled in behind him, along with a black sedan. The security officers had their guns drawn.

"Step out with your hands up."

He complied. One of the officers rushed in and put him on his knees. After checking him for a weapon, he took Phil's phone, then handcuffed him. Another man stepped out of the black sedan, walked up and flashed a badge in Phil's face. Murray from the FBI. "You are under arrested for violating the Espionage Act. You have the right to remain silent...."

Major Dalton went about his work days, not telling anyone about the assignment to be one of the test pilots for the project. The plane was coming along and the Vmax3 drive was delivered. The airframe was complete and it was just a matter of installing the engines at this point. When the general called Dalton into the office, the major already knew what it was about.

Standing in front of the general was another officer.

"Major, this is Captain Myers. He will be your copilot." Turning to the Captain, the general introduced Dalton.

"Good to meet you, Captain." Dalton looked him over. He was the young and ambitious type. He had brown hair, thin and a good two inches shorter than Dalton.

"You too, Sir."

"The captain hasn't been briefed. I was hoping you could take care of that." The general sat back down at his desk.

"Follow me, Captain." It was insane to volunteer for a project like this, especially when he had no idea what he's getting himself into. Dalton was dismayed the captain was going into this blind.

Leading the captain back to the control area, they both flashed their badges to the guards. After entering Dalton asked. "You married, Captain?"

"No, Sir, they wouldn't have let me volunteer otherwise. It was a single-man-only opportunity."

"Why did you? Volunteer, that is?"

"I'm trying to work my way up through the ranks quickly, Sir. I thought this would be a great opportunity. Not much movement in a peacetime Air Force."

The major said, "Major Dempsey, this is Captain Myers. He hasn't been briefed. Can you run the simulation for him?"

Dempsey's jaw dropped open, but he quickly shut it. "Yes, here it is. Pay particular attention to the time line at the bottom."

Myers sat there impassive until the Vmax3 drive kicked in and then his eyes widened. "There must be some mistake. The plane's going backwards in time."

"No mistake." Dempsey slowed down the simulation and landed the plane in a forested area.

"But that's impossible." The captain went pale.

"Not anymore," Dalton replied.

The captain was sweating, like he had just seen a ghost. "But?" The captain cleared his throat. "But will we be able to come back to our own time? I mean, if this thing is real?"

"We certainly hope so, but getting stuck in the past is a real possibility. The first pilot that used this drive was sent back forty-five years. He didn't make it back to the real time, but lived long enough to tell his tale."

"How far are we going to go back?"

Dalton was starting to worry about the captain. He was looking sick. "1894."

Myers looked up from the screen. "What are we supposed to be doing?"

"Letting a four-year-old Adolf Hitler drown."

"Sir?"

"Johann Kuehberger pulled a drowning Adolf Hitler from the River Inn in Passau, Germany. Our mission is to stop Johann from saving four-year-old Adolf Hitler."

"But, Sir, won't that change history?"

"Yes, it will stop the holocaust and World War Two."

"Yes, Sir." He swallowed hard.

Dalton knew the captain had the same doubts he had. Would the world be a better or a worse place because of their actions. Or did it matter at all? He didn't have time to think about it. "You will be in the back running the Vmax3 drive. I will pilot the plane. You need to become an expert on that system. Major Dempsey will show you how it works, using the simulator. I need you to get to the point that you can get us to an exact time in history within a few seconds. I don't want to end up fighting off Neanderthals."

"Yes, Sir, I understand, Sir."

The major looked him in the eye. "It would be career suicide to back out now. You and I are both stuck with this assignment. The only difference is that you volunteered. Do you have any questions?"

"Just one, Sir. The German I speak is modern. Do we know how to talk when we go back in time?"

"Colonel Ross, our historian, has worked out all of the details. He will have a handout for you as to which words you can use and which ones you can't. You will need to memorize that."

The captain swallowed hard. "Yes, Sir."

"It'll be all right, we'll get through this and make the world a better place in the process."

"I hope you're right, Sir."

Having the same doubts, Dalton understood what the captain was saying, but couldn't let on. "You'll see."

Dalton left the captain in the capable hands of Major Dempsey. Ross had narrowed down some mission specifics and he had to go over them. It was getting very near go time.

Chapter Eleven

All of the engine tests had been completed. The systems of the new plane had been checked and double checked. Except for the Vmax3 drive, everything was a go. The general didn't want to do anything with the Vmax drive until they were in the air, not knowing how the drive would react. It would give the men a chance to eject if something went wrong.

It was a cold and rainy day when they wheeled the plane out of the hanger. This would be the only test done during the day. All other tests would be done at night away from prying eyes.

Major Dalton climbed up into the cockpit. Captain Myers would not be going on this flight because the Vmax drive wasn't going to be tested yet.

The major checked his control panel. "This is Wolf, all systems normal, Control."

"Roger, Wolf, Start your engine."

"Roger."

There was a loud whining noise as the turbine began to spin. The jet roared to life. "Engine is operating normally."

"Roger, taxi your plane to the end of the runway, Wolf."

"Copy, Control."

Moving the plane slowly forward at first, Major Dalton lined it up with the white lines on the runway.

"Wolf, you are cleared to take off."

"Roger, Control."

As he throttled up the jet, the plane vibrated. He could see the white chase plane out of the corner of his eye. It would fly beside him, monitoring his every move. Releasing the brake, the plane surged forward, rapidly accelerating. When he was up to speed, he pulled back on the stick and lifted off the ground.

The feeling was exhilarating. After all that time and effort, the plane worked. His heart thundered. Despite all his misgivings of time travel, the major was ecstatic. It would only be a short flight. A simple circle of the airfield and then back down to land. He wouldn't even put the landing gear up.

He pointed the nose down and headed towards his landing. At the last minute, he would pull the nose up and touchdown.

Cheers broke out immediately from all of those watching. The side of the runway was filled with workers and engineers, everyone that had a hand in bringing the project to this moment. When the major climbed out of the plane, he was surrounded and greeted as a hero. He pumped his fist in the air. It was a great moment.

The next day, the group reported on the operation. Everything looked perfect, the flight, the airplane, and all of the systems.

Dempsey went over and over his data. It could not have gone any better.

The general walked into the room and asked the group, "Are we a go for the rest of the tests?"

Dempsey looked up from his computer. "Yes, Sir."

Over the next ten weeks, they flew the plane nearly constantly. They were testing all of the systems, especially the Vertical Takeoff and Landing (VTOL). They would not have any runways to land on when they traveled to the past, so it was critical that is was able to land and take off straight up and down.

After all systems checked out, the only thing left to run was the Vmax3 drive. The general called a meeting to figure out how best to run those tests.

"Well, gentlemen, let me first congratulate you on a job well done. The plane works wonderfully. The Boeing engineers complain that the thing's too heavy, but we keep explaining to them that it needs all the structure we've added to it. Now how do we test the drive? What are our options and what problems are we going to face?"

Major Dalton thought it was too late in the development of the airplane to be deciding these things. This should have all been settled months ago. Most of these men wanted to go home to their wives and kids after the year and a half development of the plane, but they were still here.

Dempsey spoke up. "Sir, the problem the computer model pointed out is that when running the plane backwards in time, it will land before it takes off. In the other scenario, the plane lands two hours after it took off, but the flight will only be one hour. The problem there is proving that it actually went ahead in time."

The others nodded.

"Sir," Dalton stood up. "What if we test going *forward* in time first? We can take a set time piece that has been sealed. It should be enough to prove the theory. Then when we test the backward in time scenario, we clear the runway to air traffic until the copy of the plane lands and then park it on the side, waiting for the real plane to take off."

"Is this really possible?" Colonel Ross couldn't wrap his mind around it. "Can this plane exist twice in the same time period, or will one copy of it just cease to exist and we lose two pilots?"

There was a hushed silence in the room. Captain Myers nervously bouncing the eraser from his pencil on the table.

The general squared his shoulders. "Yes, I believe it is possible. All of our computer models show it to be. We test the drive on Monday at midnight, after we fly the plane to McChord Field."

No one else commented so the meeting was over. As they walked out, Myers whispered to Dalton, "I didn't like the part about us ceasing to exist."

Dalton whispered back, "Me, either."

Chapter Tewelve

After Colonel Ross brought up the problems with having the same plane occupy the same place in two different time lines, the general came up with an idea to kill two birds with one stone. The first test would be to go forward in time, but when they ran the second test, the plane would go back in time one hour and they would fly the plane to a wooded area at Ft. Lewis to test the vertical landing. Since it would now be ahead of the actual take off, it would stay in the woods until word came down the runway was clear, then they would take off and return to base to McChord to land.

Everyone was satisfied with this approach.

Captain Myers took the controls of the Vmax3 drive, with Major Dalton in front of him in the tandem cockpit, ready to roll. When the all clear was given, they throttled up the plane and took off. Gaining altitude up to twenty thousand feet, Dalton leveled off the plane. "Control, this is Wolf. We are ready to engage the drive."

"Roger, Wolf. Engage the drive."

Myers took a deep breath, then set the drive time feature for one hour forward and flipped the switch. A loud whining noise ensued and the plane buffeted, then shook violently, but when the drive disengaged, the flight smoothed back out.

"That was wild, Sir." Myers checked his controls. "Everything is normal. Time is 01:22pm per both my watch and the internal timer."

"Control, this is Wolf, doing a time check."

"Wolf, the time is now 02:22."

"Roger, Control, our time in the flight deck is 01:22."

Dalton could hear cheering in the background. "Roger, Wolf."

When he brought the plane around and landed, a group of cheering men rushed out to surround Captain Myers and Major Dalton. At one point, they even had Dalton on their shoulders, but he wasn't liking it. He asked to get down.

They walked into the conference room that had been set up at the air field as a control center. The general was waiting for them with big smile. "Well done, gentlemen. We have made history today. It's all of you who have made this moment possible. I'm giving everyone tomorrow off because of the lateness of the hour, but we will need to get here that much earlier the next day to prepare for the next set of tests."

Everyone cheered again and filed out. Major Dalton was the last to leave. He sent a quick email to Dempsey, and turned out the lights on his way out.

The plane was fueled and ready to go when Dalton arrived at the control center two days later. Dempsey took him to the side as soon as he saw him. "I got your email. The buffeting is due to the drive kicking it. It goes opposite of the jet engine so the two of them are counteracting each other. It shouldn't be as bad when you go back in time as it is going forward because the engine and the drive will be spinning the same way."

"Will it be that bad every time I go forward in time?"

"I'm afraid so, but the plane was designed to handle the stresses, so you'll be okay."

"I nearly lost control of it, to tell you the truth. I'll be expecting it next time so I'll be prepared."

"I thought you were warned. It was in all of the models we ran."

Dalton thought for a minute. "Now that I reflect on it, I knew about it, just didn't expect it to be so bad."

"You handled it well. You brought the plane back in one piece."

"Yes, luckily. When's today's test?"

"You have one hour."

Dalton smiled. "Well, I had better get my flight suit on then. Is Captain Myers here?"

"He's ready to go."

Dalton strapped himself into the cockpit. This test had him the most worried. Being trapped in the past was his worst nightmare. *One hour, it's only one hour.*

Myers was behind him ready, to engage the Vmax3 drive. This was the true test. If this didn't work, everything would have been in vain. All the money and time would be wasted. He sat there with the engine on and waiting at the edge of the runway.

"Wolf, you are cleared for takeoff and Godspeed."

"Thank you, Control." He throttled up and released the brake. The plane rumbled down the runway and lifted gracefully into the air.

When he was at twenty thousand feet, he leveled off. "This is Wolf, we are ready to engage the drive."

"Roger, Wolf, you are cleared to do so."

"Here goes everything," Myers said as he activated the drive.

The plane started accelerating rapidly, but Dalton had expected that and throttled back. When Myers disengaged the drive, he throttled forward again. "Well, how did we do?"

"I don't know. We're not supposed to contact Control until we take off again." Dalton thought about how strange it sounded. He was waiting for himself to take off.

He looked for the designated landing spot. Finding it, he pulled back the throttle to a hover, slowly bringing the plane down. It was touch and go, as the weight of the plane was making the engine strain as he came down. There was a crew in the woods to verify the landing and make sure the plane wasn't damaged, a squad of soldiers and two mechanics. The mechanics gave the plane a quick inspection.

After verifying that everything was good, the Army lieutenant said, "You're going to have to wait here until I get the all clear. Apparently, there is another plane on the runway. It has to take off before I can allow you to go back to the airbase."

Dalton stared at him. The lieutenant didn't know what was going on, but what he was saying told Dalton the mission had been a complete success. He heart skipped a beat. His had gone back in time.

Myers was all smiles as he looked down from the cockpit at the Army officer. "Sure, no problem, we'll wait here." Myers smacked the major on his shoulder. "Won't we, Sir?"

Dalton smiled. "Never did want to get back too early."

Around an hour later, the lieutenant gave them the all clear. The 'other' plane had taken off.

Dalton throttled up the engines and the airplane slowly rose straight up into the air. As he pushed it forward, it gained speed, soaring into the sky. He saw the airbase below them. "This is Wolf, Control, we are coming in."

"Roger, Wolf, you are cleared to land."

"Roger."

Again when the plane was on the ground and secured, there was the cheering mass surrounding them as Dalton and Myers climbed out of the plane.

Chapter Thirteen

It was to be the final test. The plan was to take off, go back 100 years in time to 1941, land in a secluded area, change clothes and walk into town, then buy a newspaper. When they took off again, they would fly forward in time 100 years, landing an hour after they took off. It would be the first time they practiced for the actual mission.

Anticipation was high. *A hundred years*, Dalton thought, *I won't live long enough to make it back to the real time if this fails.* He thought about R. Adalwolf Dalton house in the Hamptons. It was built before 1942.

Dalton and Myers sat at breakfast as the mechanics did the last checks on the airplane. As he ate, the major looked over at the captain. "I want to dispense with military formality during this mission and the rest of the time we are working together. I don't want you to call me sir. From now on, you call me Robert. I will call you Gerald. I don't want us slipping up at all."

"Yes, Si…, I mean, yes Robert."

"I know, it will take some getting used to."

The general came in with Colonel Ross. He went right to the point. "Men, the plane is ready. I wanted to personally wish you good luck on this mission. All of our hopes are riding on your success."

The colonel added, "I have some money from the late thirties. Should be enough to buy a newspaper and get something to eat, if you feel so inclined. I personally would love to come with you."

"Yes, Sir, thank you, Sir." Pocketing the money, the two men headed out to the airplane.

Dalton felt the anticipation when he taxied toward the runway. He was sweating. Anxiety had hit him. He was having flashbacks to his crash. Taking deep breaths, he was able to calm down.

"You okay, Sir?" Myers asked.

"Just pre-flight jitters. Let's do this."

"Yes, Sir."

Takeoff was smooth as he pulled back on the yoke. Soon they had reached their cruising altitude. "This is Wolf. We are at 35,000 feet."

"Roger, Wolf, engage drive when you are ready."

"Roger, Control." Dalton took a deep breath. "Let her rip, Gerald."

The plane accelerated rapidly as the second engine pushed them forward, causing the major to pull back on the throttle. Twenty minutes later, the drive disengaged. Dalton looked down at the Seattle landscape. They flashed past forests that would all be cut down for urban sprawl in the future.

"Do you think they can track us?"

"No, not well. Their radar was very rudimentary at this point in history."

"I hope so. Find us a spot to touch down."

There were plenty of woods around, so they found a clearing in a secluded forest next to a major road. As the plane touched down, Dalton and Myers grabbed their pistols and scouted out the area to be sure they weren't spotted. Feeling safe, they went back to the plane and opened the storage bay. It had a camouflage covering for the plane and two suits for them to wear into town. Taking off their flight gear, they donned the clothes.

After securing the plane with the cover, they made their way to the road.

"What are we supposed to do, hail a cab, Sir… I mean, Robert?"

"Stick your thumb out, People were more trusting in this day and age."

It wasn't long before a motorist stopped. A man in a white hat driving a black Packard.

"What are you fellows doing in the woods this late at night?"

"Our car ran off the road. We just need a ride into town to get a tow truck."

"Glad to help, hop on in."

They both sat in the back and the driver turned around from time to time to talk to them. "You from around here? You have an eastern accent."

"No, I'm from New Jersey, came out here with the Air Force. I'm hoping to fight against the Japanese."

"A lot of our young men are signing up. Terrible thing, them attacking Pearl Harbor and all. Where can I drop you?"

"At the local diner."

"Nothing open at this time of night."

"Is there a hotel nearby?"

"Sure, sure." He drove up to the Olympic Hotel. "You have a good night."

"Thanks for the ride."

Myers admired the tall structure, dominating the skyline for blocks around. It was a brick structure that went up about twenty stories. Large white stones made up the base of the nearly square hotel.

Dalton led the way, through the wood-paneled lobby. It was two stories tall and full of fine furniture and large, wooden pillars. As he walked up to the desk, Myers rested his arm on the counter.

"How can I help you gentlemen?" The desk clerk smiled. "That's a fancy watch you have on. Is that numbers on it? I've never seen anything like it."

Horrified, Myers realized he forgot to change out his digital watch for the one Colonel Ross had given them. 'No, uh, it's just a toy. A gag gift."

"Oh, can I see it?"

Dalton cut in. "I'm sorry, but we need a room. It's late and we need some rest. Is there a place to get a newspaper around here?"

"I have a copy of yesterday's. The paper doesn't come out until the morning."

"Yesterday's paper would be fine."

The man handed them one. "That will be five cents, oh, and six dollars for the room."

Dalton handed him a ten and waited for his change.

"No bags?" the clerk asked.

"No, we travel light."

"Have a good night." The clerk handed them a key. "Can I have you sign the registry?"

After signing they walked around the lobby. Myers was apologetic. "I forgot about the watch, Sir, I mean Robert."

"Don't worry about it."

"Why did we get a room?"

"We're not staying. I wanted to sign the registry and maybe have Colonel Ross look it up."

"Oh, okay."

They headed out the front door. The doorman greeted them.

"Can you call us a cab?"

"Yes, of course, Sir."

A few minutes later the cab pulled up. Dalton handed the door man the room key before getting in.

The cab driver was smoking a cigar and the whole car was filled with fumes. "Where're you heading?"

"Drive north on 99 until we tell you to stop."

The man shook his head and then puffed the cigar a couple of times. Myers was turning green so Dalton cracked open his window. When they arrived at the corner where they had left the plane, Dalton had the driver stop. He paid him.

"There's nothing around here. What are you guys doing this far out?"

"Farmhouse, down the road," Dalton said, but he knew it wasn't convincing.

The driver shook his head again and drove off.

Chapter Fourteen

An hour later the plane had landed. Cheers greeted the pilots even before they reported in. Dalton and Myers were treated like heroes wherever they went and today was no different. When they climbed out of the plane, they were escorted up to the control room where they were debriefed.

The first thing Major Dalton did was throw the newspaper on the table. "Mission accomplished."

This brought another round of cheers from the assembled group. The general and Senator James were all smiles. Colonel Ross looked at the hot-off-the-press paper. "It's the exact date we were aiming for."

Senator James entered the room. "Gentlemen, congratulations on your success. We have proven the system works. Next stop, the eradication of Hitler and preventing the holocaust."

Another cheer went up in the room. Only Major Dalton wasn't cheering. He took exception to the word *eradication*. He had been in the military a long time and never had to kill anyone yet. He didn't like the idea of doing it now. It wasn't that he was going to pull the trigger, but he was going to cause the death of a four-year-old little boy and he was not okay with that. He knew the senator's wife had some ancestors who were killed in a concentration camp, and that was why James was so obsessed with killing Hitler.

When the cheering died down, he forced a smile, he didn't want his thoughts to be obvious.

The general brought the pilots into his office, followed by Colonel Ross, who was still carrying the newspaper.

When they were all sat down the general pelted them with questions. "Did everything seem normal?"

"They were all on a war footing and wondering what two men of military age were doing, wandering around in the night," Dalton replied.

Myers leaned back into the corner of the room. He seemed happy just to listen to the debriefing, not wanting to add anything unless he was specifically asked.

"Did you run into any trouble?"

"No, it seemed fairly routine. We landed, walked to the highway and caught a ride into town. The restaurants were all closed, so we didn't get anything to eat. I did sign the guest register at the hotel. I thought Colonel Ross might be able to track that."

Ross nodded, "I'll see what I can find."

"When we were done, we took a taxi back to where we had hidden the airplane."

Myers added, "The taxi driver thought we were crazy, I think, but he didn't say much."

"You didn't affect the time line in any way, do you think?"

"No, Sir. We were very professional in everything we did," Myers replied.

"Good, good to hear it." Turning to Ross, the general asked. "Do you have anything else?"

"No, not at this time."

"Gentlemen, go get some rest. When you come back tomorrow, we will work on the final plan for the first real mission. Operation Hitler. We will be able to affect more positive changes in the world after that."

"Yes, Sir." Dalton said, then he and Myers saluted and left the room.

As they walked down the stairs to their cars, Myers said. "That went well, they seemed to be pleased."

"Yes, we did good."

"I wonder what they will have us do after we take care of Hitler."

Dalton thought for a moment. "I hadn't thought of that. I guess, step by step, we'll create a perfect world. A perfect world for America, that is. It might not be so perfect for our enemies."

"Wow, we could be the two most important people in history," Myers said.

"Only problem is, our missions will always be classified at the highest level, so none of our enemies will ever know that we're manipulating their history. Imagine, the two most unknown people in history who will have had the greatest effect on it."

Myers turned to Dalton, "Okay, you win, I'll never be famous. Call me a secret agent. Maybe a secret history manipulator. I could be okay with that."

"Sure, if it makes you happy. What will make me happy is to have this mission over with. Maybe they will need to take out Stalin next. They will need two Russian speaking pilots so we'll be off the hook."

"Or maybe they send us to a Russian course and have us do it. I don't trust these guys to just let us walk away."
Dalton sighed, "You're probably right. We'll be doing this until we're old and gray."

Myers chuckled, "And when we're too old, they'll go back in time and get our younger selves and start over."

Dalton laughed even though it wasn't funny.

When Dalton arrived at work the next morning, Colonel Ross handed him a piece of paper. "You actually caused a minor stir during your visit to the past. The taxi driver called the cops on you. Two suspicious German-looking men were seen along the road into Seattle."

Dalton looked over the photocopy of the old archived newspaper. "What should we do?"

"That's the beauty of time travel, you can go back and back until you get everything perfect. I showed the general the article. He didn't think it was important enough to send you back to fix it. It did bring out an interesting point, though. What can we do to get you into town without relying on taxis, or hitching a ride?"

Dalton shrugged his shoulders. He didn't know history well enough to even venture a guess.

"Bicycles. We are going to supply you with two of them. They will look and ride like turn-of-the-nineteenth-century models, but will be collapsible, to fit inside the storage area on your plane. That was my idea."

"The storage area is going to be very crowded."

"Yes, unfortunately it is. We will have time to expand it a bit, since the bikes are going to take weeks to manufacture. Your mission is delayed."

Dalton shook his head. He had hoped to have it over and done with.

"It doesn't matter when you go. Time has already happened. It can wait to happen again." Ross reminded him.

Chapter Fifteen

The oil tank had to be moved. It was forward of the Vmax3 drive. The designers came up with the idea of bending and splitting it. Putting the new tank on either side of the drive, like saddle bags on a horse. The engineers warned this would cause the oil to heat up more, but it would still be within acceptable levels as long as they kept the tanks near full.

This allowed the team to push the wall of the storage container back, allowing room for the new bikes.

The mission had been planned to the minute. The major problem was they didn't know the exact day that Hitler was saved, so they had to estimate. Otherwise, it would go off without a hitch.

Step one would be to fly the plane to Erding Air Base, between Passau and Munich. Refuel there, they would take off again and travel back in time to January 1894. They would land in a clearing just south of town. Riding the bikes to a place along the River Inn, they would wait for Hitler to fall in and then prevent Johann Kuehberger from rescuing him. Then they would travel forward in time and land at Erding again. There they would Refuel and then fly back home. The general didn't want to wait too long for the return, so the plane would travel forward in time on its final leg. They were scheduled to be home early the next morning.

The general, himself, wanted to show off the new bikes. He wheeled one of them into the conference room. "This, gentlemen, is your new ride. It's funny that you will step out of a billion dollar plane and onto an 1800s bicycle." He smiled. "It looks exactly like the ones from that century. The only difference is it's collapsible." He unscrewed the front and the back and pushed the bike together. It wasn't much larger than the two tires that overlapped each other. "This will be the most expensive bicycle of the century. I mean, that century anyway."

Dalton looked closer. He pulled on the two tires and the bike went back to its usable form. He then screwed the front and the back and he had a normal-looking bike. "Wow, that's great."

"Yes, just don't leave these behind. They are of modern materials. It would send bicycle manufacturing light years ahead of what they should be, history wise."

"Yes, Sir," Myers said.

Dalton looked at him and wondered what he was being so enthusiastic about. He finally realized the only reason Myers had volunteered for this project was to get rank advancement.

Dalton called it the last supper, although not in front of the general. The crew and technical staff all came together for dinner the evening before the early morning departure. The computers and monitors had all been moved aside from the main table in the conference room. Honey baked ham, a large turkey, fried chicken and all sorts of side dishes made up the feast. Everyone took their plates and piled them high, then sat around the table and visited while they ate. Myers sat down next to Dalton.

"What do you think our chances are?"

Dalton turned. "I'm thinking around zero percent. I sure hope, for our sakes, I'm wrong."

Myers' eyes widened. "If you thought it was hopeless, why did you volunteer?"

"I didn't."

"Oh." Myers looked down at his plate.

"Eat. Take advantage of the moment. You won't see a spread like this again for a long time. I'm just being a pessimist. All of the other tests went fine."

"I guess you're right. You took me by surprise, is all."

"Sorry," he said with a smile, but in his heart he felt a deep hopelessness.

The general came up. "Well, you two. Are you excited? You get to change history tomorrow. No one's ever done that before."

Myers mustered some enthusiasm. "Yes, Sir. Thank you for this opportunity, Sir."

Dalton smiled and nodded, pretending his mouth was full, but it wasn't.

"Best of luck to both of you. I'm already filling out the paperwork for your commendations. I'm sure they will go through without a hitch when you get back. Imagine, saving millions of lives. It gives me goose bumps just thinking about it." The general walked away without waiting for them to comment.

Chapter Sixteen

The day had finally arrived. The general brought in a military band for the occasion. Unlike the tests, the real mission would take off in broad daylight. Senator James was there, along with a few ranking officers. To those not in the program, it was just a lot of ceremony for that ugly new plane they had built. It was the first time many of the airmen at the base had seen the 'top secret' plane. Its purpose was not plain to anyone there. The rumors were it was the fastest plane in the sky, being able to go mach five. After seeing it, however, it was obvious to even the most casual observer, it wasn't made for speed. The smaller engine on top was situated where it would cause a lot of drag.

"Control, this is Wolf. All systems are operational."

"Roger, Wolf, taxi out to runway 33."

"Roger, Control."

Major Dalton fired up the engine. He felt guilty about telling Myers that there was no hope for success. He should have kept his opinion to himself. Myers had been very quiet this morning, not even smiling for the pictures. The general wanted every aspect of this momentous day recorded. He was overjoyed the Holocaust would no longer be in the history books, if he succeeded.

To Dalton, the plane felt heavy as it moved down the taxiway. He knew the two bikes wouldn't have added that much weight, but the reworking of the plane made it react differently. His heart thundered as he lined up with the end of the runway.

"Wolf, this is Control. You are cleared for takeoff. Godspeed."

"Roger, Control."

He revved up the engine and released the brakes. The plane launched forward and gained speed. He pulled back on the yoke and it was airborne.

General William felt a surge of pride. Soon he would have another major project brought to a successful completion. The plane worked. He wondered how changing time would affect things. Would he even know what he had accomplished? If time changed, would it alter his reality of events, or would he just look in the history books and see that the holocaust disappeared? He wondered about a lot of things as the plane faded from sight.

Applause broke out all around him. He looked around. They were applauding him. "Thank you, gentlemen. You have done a wonderful job. You should be applauding yourselves, not me."

The men all shook each other's hands and then the group dispersed. The band began packing up their instruments. It had been a great day so far. Going home, he had left word for the base to keep him posted.

The next morning, when the general made it back to his office, Colonel Ross was already there, waiting for him.

"Well, how do you think this will all play out?"

"Sir, I see one of two things happening. Either those men will be heroes when they get back, or a plane will land and we'll wonder whose plane it is."

The general sat down. "I hadn't thought of that. I hope we know what we have accomplished here. If we don't know anything about the plane, then the Senator will have my hide for spending all of that money."

"Or did you spend the money? We could be affected so many different ways with all of this. You might not even be in the military in this new reality."

"Now you're giving me a headache with all these theories."

"Yes, Sir." Ross stood up. "I'm going to get something to eat. Do you care to join me?"

"No, thank you. I'm going to sit here until the plane returns. I want to be the first one down there when they get back."

"Suit yourself, Sir." Ross walked out the door.

The general pulled out the history book he kept in his drawer, the one Ross had given for Christmas a few years back. He opened it to the holocaust. *Hmm, it's still there.* He sat there waiting for the book to change.

Two hours had past and still no word from the airplane. The general went up to the control tower. The men were monitoring the radar.

"No sign of them?" All of the outbound reports had come in. The plane had landed at Gabreski Airport in New York on schedule. Erding Air Base in Germany had reported them ahead of schedule. Refueled, the plane had taken off, flew below the radar level and disappeared. It was all according to plan. The German base had been told that the plane would practice its vertical landing in one of its many forests. When the mission was complete, they would reappear, as expected, then land and refuel.

"No, Sir. Erding says they took off two hours ago, but haven't returned. Do we call out a search and rescue mission yet, Sir?"

"Not yet, there could be a slight delay." The General's heart sank. They should have been back. *Did they disappear in the current time, or in the past?* He paced back and forth.

An hour later Senator James came on the base. Williams went down to talk to him.

The senator was blunt. "My history book says the holocaust still happened. I see yours does, too. Did your time machine fail?"

"I don't know yet, but I am monitoring the situation."

The senator's face reddened. "If this mission fails, I will hang you out to dry. We are talking congressional investigation and court martial. Do you understand me? They will want to know where all the money has gone." By this point the senator was so close the general could feel the warmth of his breath.

"Let me remind you, Senator James is just as guilty, if that's the correct word, as I am. I have two men out there I'm worried about and all you can think of is the money?"

"I don't care if I go down with you, you will go down one way or another." James stomped out of the office. The general was glad to see him go.

Chapter Seventeen

It was six months to the day that the Air Force pulled the plug on the project. The plane never showed back up and no trace of it was ever found. Despite his threats, Senator James didn't call for an investigation. The matter was handled quietly, with General Williams' sudden retirement.

Colonel Ross was put in charge of the project with the sole purpose of shutting it down. Major Dempsey was also kept on. Running different scenarios on the modeling computer, he tried to figure out what the possibilities were. It was an impossible task, because he had no data. He felt that the only reason he was actually there was to keep Ross company.

It should have been an easy thing to kill the project, but Ross kept it open. He studied history books to see if the project had made any unintended impacts. He kept looking for unexplained planes and UFOs around the intended time of the mission. He couldn't find anything.

One morning Major Dempsey was running yet another unneeded model. This time he was projecting the impact on history, had the airplane had turned up in a forest around 1900. He watched the colonel go through newspapers from around that time also. Suddenly Ross' normally glum expression changed into a smile. This caught Dempsey's attention. The colonel became more animated. He started typing rapidly into the computer. When he brought up one particular screen, Ross laughed loud and long.

"Are you all right, Sir?"

Ross laughed so hard that tears were forming in his eyes. When he finally caught his breath, he stood bolt upright and ran over to the file cabinet. He pulled out one of the personnel files, then coming back to his desk he compared it to the file on the computer screen. "It was there all along. I'm so stupid. It couldn't have been more obvious."

"Sir?"

Ross turned to Dempsey. "Where is the best place to hide something?"

"I don't know, Sir."

"In plain sight. I found Dalton."

"Excuse me, Sir?"

"I don't have time to explain. I have to get to the FBI forensic lab right away." The colonel printed out the file on the computer, then took out the door, leaving a bewildered Major, still sitting at his desk.

Not knowing what else to do, Major Dempsey kept rerunning the model. After a few minutes he went to the filing cabinet and looked to see whose personal file was missing. It was Dalton's. *He has found him.*

The next morning, Dempsey was at the office early. He had started yet another needless model when the colonel came in.

"Shut that down. You have been reassigned back to DC. You get to go home to your wife and family."

Dempsey was dumbfounded. "Today, Sir?"

"Yes, this very minute. I am having a team come in and shut down the project once and for all. The hard drives will be taken out and archived, along with all the plans and schematics of the airplane and Vmax3 drive. If it were up to me, I would burn all of this so no one ever looked at it again. It was a stupid idea, messing with history. We could've destroyed our very existence."

"You said you found Major Dalton, Sir?"

The colonel looked Dempsey in the eye. "I did, but I can't talk about it. The less people know the better."

"Is he okay, Sir? That's all I want to know."

The colonel shook his head slowly back and forth. "There is no way to answer that question without giving you a lot more information than you want to know. This whole project is going under wraps. It will be hidden in the farthest corner of the archives and hopefully never again see the light of day."

"Yes, Sir." Dempsey picked up the papers he was working on and handed them to Ross. "It has been good working for you, Sir."

The colonel let out a sigh, then shook his hand. "I don't have all the answers I need yet, but someday, you and I are going to take a long walk in the park, far from any listening ears. I will tell you an amazing story. I promise."

"Yes, Sir. Thank you, Sir." Dempsey smiled as he headed out the door. It had all been so sudden, but it was good that Ross was finally on the right track.

Two days later Dempsey was home with his family.

Chapter Eighteen

Lieutenant General Aston Williams USAF (Retired), the label read. Williams opened the packet. It was his final paperwork. *They let me keep my rank and pension, at least.* He thought, while thumbing through the file. With a sigh, he put it down and picked up his novel.

He had finished the house. The den had deep blue carpeting and cream colored walls. The fireplace had a stone façade and was lit. The fire's glow created shadows in the room and the wood crackled and spit as it burned. Aston had turned his recliner towards the flames. It warmed his toes as he read.

None of his old Air Force friends would have anything to do with him, those who were still trying to make rank, anyway. It didn't matter to him. He was going to make the most of his retirement. Now that the house was complete, he planned on doing some traveling. Tonight was all about a good book and a warm fire.

He heard the door bell ring, as it did most nights around this time. Caroline had made lots of friends during the time he was away and they were always getting together to go shopping or having a ladies night out. He was happy she had kept busy. She seemed to take the whole collapse of his career in stride. She enjoyed having him around.

Deep inside, he felt that he had disgraced the family name, but she and his father didn't seem the least bothered by his troubles.

Aston looked up as Caroline escorted Colonel Ross into the room.

"Someone to see you, Honey." She left the room to give the two of them their privacy.

Ross nodded, "General, don't get up. You look so comfortable."

"Please, call me Aston. What brings you to the Hamptons? Trying to ruin your career by associating with me?"

The colonel chuckled. "My career? I can't wait to get out of the service. I'm counting the days. No, I have some business to attend to."

"I see. This wouldn't happen to do with any projects we worked on together?"

"Yes, it would, strictly off the record, of course. I need to put it to bed, but I have just one last thread to follow."

"Of course, off the record. What do you have?"

"Major Dalton asked me to follow up to see if he was related to the builder of this house. In my spare time, of course. I was so busy with the project I set it on the back burner and focused on finding what happened to the plane. It turns out, he was giving me a hint. A large hint. I should have done what he asked first."

William's eyebrows rose. "Go on."

"Remember that night when we were all together at a dinner party here, and I mentioned that R. Adalwolf Dalton had built this house?"

"Vaguely."

"Major Dalton's middle name was Adalwolf."

Tingles went up Aston's spine. "What are you saying?"

"I'm saying that Dalton knew he was going to get stuck back in time. He knew all along, but didn't say anything to anybody, except me. I was going to be the one to try and find him, so he gave me a hint of where to look."

"Major Dalton built this house?" His voice betrayed his astonishment more than he wanted it to.

The colonel moved the coffee table to in front of the general. He pulled up a chair next to Aston's and opened up his briefcase. Pulling out some papers, he laid two photographs on the table.

"This first one is R. Adalwolf Dalton, the man who built this house. This second photo is of Major Robert Adalwolf Dalton. Adalwolf is the name his mother gave him. She was German. He knew it would stand out, so he used that instead of the more common name Robert. When he heard the name at the dinner party, he knew what was about to happen, I suppose.

"If you look at the photos, you will see they are very similar. I had the FBI forensics lab do a digital comparison on the faces. They concluded that these photos are of the same man. I toyed with the idea of digging up the body to do a DNA analysis, but decided against it."

"Dalton built this house?" Aston shook his head in disbelief. "What, is that important? Why would he do that?"

"It gets worse. I researched the house and found a complaint filed by the neighbors about a strange design on his chimney." Ross handed him another photo. The chimney had white bricks incorporated into it. The shapes looked like large arrows pointing downward. They started at the top and went all the way to the ground. After his death, the chimney was bricked over to hide the white arrows."

The general was trying to figure out what he was saying.

"Here's a picture of R. Adalwolf Dalton's head stone. Notice the writing on the bottom, below the date."

Aston read it out loud. "A hole in time, beneath the hearth." He glanced at his warm fire, and then back to the pictures. "The chimney has to come down, doesn't it?"

"Yes, I think that is where the final report of the Black Hole Project is. I learned a lot about R. Adalwolf Dalton. He was a financier, investing heavily in munitions manufacturers at the turn of the century. The First World War made him a millionaire. The Second World War made him even richer. He died soon after the end of it, leaving behind a wife and two sons."

Williams smiled. "He finally married?"

"Yes."

"Tonight I'm going to enjoy my nice warm fire. Tomorrow, I will rent a wrecking ball and start demolishing my chimney."

Chapter Nineteen

"I still don't understand, why are we doing this?" Caroline clutched her coat around her to ward off the winter chill. They stood outside in the snow watching the workmen knocking the bricks down.

"It's all top secret. I can't tell you why."

"Top secret!" she screeched. "You're not even in the service anymore."

Ross was smiling to himself at Aston's predicament. He had come to watch the proceedings. The Colonel had decided that the document was the general's personal property, so he wouldn't have to archive it with all the other things he was trying to hide. It would be easier that way. His report would show the project was an abject failure so no one would ever try again.

When the workmen finally cleared the last of the bricks away from the foundation of the chimney, there etched in the cement was a large letter.

"X marks the spot." Aston said.

"Mrs. Williams, I'm sorry, but I must insist that you go inside for the next part of this."

"Colonel Ross, this is my home that you are demolishing. I at least intend to find out why."

"Please."

She sighed, shook her head, and walked away. The jackhammer started in on the cement. Soon the corner of a metal box was visible in the bits and pieces of the foundation.

"There it is." He sounded like a school boy who had just found his favorite ball in the toy closet.

The workman was careful not to damage the box, but worked his way around it, uncovering the edges until the entire thing was visible. "What is it?" he asked.

"A time capsule, just a bunch of really old papers." Ross replied.

The man nodded. "Okay, guys, let's clean up this mess and then be on our way."

The general carefully lifted the heavy metal box out of its hole. Ross followed him as they brought it into the house. Walking past a frowning Caroline, they went into the living room. He set the box on the floor and sat down. Ross did too. The two men gently opened it.

Inside were two hard bound books, both in German, and a binder with paperwork in it.

"My heart's racing," Aston put his hand to his chest. "What do we do with all this stuff?"

"I think we take it to my office and go through it. I'll need a translator or two to see what these books say anyway. What's in the binder?"

Aston Williams gently opened it, blew the dust off and read the title page. "Final report of Project Black Hole, completed March 11, 1912." Williams looked up at Ross. "This is it, this is really it." His voice was giddy. "It worked after all."

"We'll see. I'll take everything, but I promise not to read it until you're there in the room. Meanwhile, I'll get these books translated. All this is top secret and must never be told to anyone."

"Of course."

Ross put everything back in the box. "Thanks for destroying your chimney. You didn't have to you, know. I'll get you a check for the damages."

"Yes, I did have to. Those were my guys. At least now I'll know what happened to them."

Ross smiled. "Goodnight."

The general walked him to the door.

Major Dempsey enjoyed his month-long furlough. He and his wife drove down the coast, and reconnected. He was surprised when his orders came in. He was still assigned to Colonel Ross.

Dutifully, he reported. It was a Monday morning and yet another dusting of snow was on the ground in Washington, DC as he drove to the office.

"There you are," Ross said as Dempsey entered the room.

"Reporting as ordered, Sir."

"I have the final report here of Project Black Hole. I thought you would like to be here for the reading of it."

"Yes, Sir. Very much, Sir. I was hoping to find out what happened."

A man in civilian dress entered the room. He looked over to see who it was. "General?"

"Please, call me Aston." He turned to Ross. "This is it, then?"

"Yes, I put all the pages in sheet protectors. The old papers were a little brittle. I also have the translations of the two books that were in the packet. No one outside of this room will ever hear what this report contains. Please close the door."

Major Ross started reading aloud.

Chapter Twenty

Final Report of Project Black Hole, Completed March 11, 1912. Submitted by Major Robert Adalwolf Dalton.

I wasn't going to write this report. At first I was bitter at being stuck in the wrong time. Now I'm married to a wonderful woman and have a son, with another child on the way. I've calmed down. Since we are adding a wing to the house, I will place this in the foundation of the chimney, with the hopes it'll be found someday. It has taken me months to write, but I felt Colonel Ross would want to know everything that happened. I have written it down in detail.

Under orders not to use the Vmax3 drive until we reached Germany, we flew for four and a half hours to Otis Air National Guard base on the east coast. We refueled there. Since we had another long flight to go, we spent the night at the base, as the general had arranged. We checked the plane. It seemed heavier, maybe a little sluggish, but found it to be in perfect working order. I have to admit, I was hoping that there were problems with it, so we could scrub the mission.

The next morning, we flew to Erding Air Base in Germany. The Germans refueled the plane and we were on the ground less than an hour. I wondered what alarms we were going to set off when the plane went back in time and disappeared from their radar. What General Williams had in mind, I don't know, but I suppose he had a rehearsed story to explain away the anomaly.

Myers was cautiously optimistic, but I had a premonition that it would all go horribly wrong…

Passau Germany 1894

As the Vmax3 drive shut off, the plane's violent vibrations stopped. Checking the gauges, Myers reported, "Sir, we have arrived at the right time and day."

Night had fallen and Dalton looked down at the lights of the city. It wasn't like a modern city where the street lights would illuminate large areas, but the flickering of the pale gas lamps lit up small areas of the town. He selected a clearing in a forested area, away from any lights, to set the plane down. All efforts had been made to keep the plane as quiet as possible, but it was still loud when it took off and landed due to the strain of the engine. When they finally rested on solid ground, both men took out their pistols and hopped out of the plane.

Searching the woods for any sign of alarm from the locals, they found they were alone.

Dalton took a deep breath. "Well, this is it. We're here." *If we can only get back now.*

"Yes, Sir." Myers replied.

"Don't call me, Sir. I'm your friend, Robert. Remember that."

"Yes, of course. Old habit, I'm afraid."

The two men changed clothes and then dug the camouflage netting out of the cargo hold and strung it over the airplane.

Assembling their bikes, they headed into town. The streets were narrow and the cobblestone jarred them as they rode along. The wind almost blew off Myers' hat several times. It looked like a bolo hat. He felt ridiculous wearing it, but was assured by Colonel Ross, it was all the rage during the late 1890s. The men peddled close to the old wall of the city.

"Let's stop here until daybreak. It'll look highly suspicious having two men enter the city during the night." Dalton stepped off his bike and laid it in the undergrowth, near a tree.

"Are we walking into town, then, Robert?"

Dalton looked at him for a second then said, "Yes, Gerald, we are walking into town."

"I could call you Robert the Red."

"I think not. Besides it would be, Robert der Rot."

"Yeah, you're right, I'll stick with Robert."

"A very good idea, Captain."

"Yes, Sir. I mean, yes, Robert." Myers place his bike alongside Dalton's. They both sat back against the tree until the sun came up. There was surprisingly little snow on the ground for January, but the air was cold. Myers buttoned up his coat and drew his knees in to keep warm. Two hours later, the sun was just peeking over the horizon when the two men got up to start their walk into the city.

Chapter Twenty-One

They walked along Ludwig's Bridge, over the Inn River. It was a wooden structure, but sound and offered them a good vantage point to where they could see what was happening on the promenade that ran along the far bank of the river. Knowing that they had at least one more day before the actual event, Dalton looked for a hotel to stay in. Ross hadn't been able to pinpoint the exact date of Hitler's near drowning, so the two of them might have to be there several days. They walked towards the large St. Stephen's Cathedral with white spires and green onion shaped domes on top. Above it, on a hill that overshadowed the Danube River sat a group of large white buildings.

"What do you think that is?" Myers asked as he looked up.

"You didn't do your homework about Passau?"

"I did study the maps, but just about the part of the city that lies between the rivers. I didn't go outside the city further than that. I didn't think I needed it."

Dalton smiled, "Very well, that is what is currently known as Veste Oberhaus, it started out as a fortress for the local bishops under the Holy Roman Empire. It was turned over to the Bavarian government. In 1918, it will become a prison, then later a museum and youth hostel."

"Wow, busy building."

"It's been there since the early 1200s."

"I should have studied more. I thought this was going to be a quick in and out though."

Dalton stopped smiling and turned to Myers. "I don't know about you, but I have a premonition that I'm not going to make it back to our own time. That's why I did all of the extra research. I've figured out how I'm going back to the United States. I'll book first class passage back through Cherbourg, France. Ellis Island didn't mind letting the rich in. It was the poor they hesitated on. I've got enough German money for the train, and the steam ship."

Myers looked dumbfounded. "You really thought this out. I wish you would have included me in all this. How am I going to get back to America, if we fail?"

Letting out a brief laugh, Dalton replied, "Don't worry, I won't leave you behind."

"Good."

When they came to the end of the bridge, they walked up the street, past a large opera house, away from the promenade and found a room in a hotel.

The sunlight through the windows lit up the space. There was one large bed and three overstuffed chairs. The floor was wood with throw rugs on it. The room was cold, so Dalton took out some wood and lit a fire in the fireplace.

"No lights," Myers noted.

"Lanterns only." Dalton looked out the window. "I can't see the river from here. We'll have to find a place closer to observe the children playing."

"I saw a theater on the way in. It looked like it had a café next door to it."

"That will have to do."

Myers looked around. "No bathroom?"

"You really didn't read the briefing that Colonel Ross wrote, did you?"

"I skimmed it." He sounded defensive. "History isn't my thing."

"You should have made it your thing, because you're now in the middle of it. You have two options. The first is the chamber pot, which I hope you don't use because we'll be smelling it all night. The other is the little house out back."

"We couldn't have waited until the toilet was invented? Hitler lived many years."

Dalton smiled, "The toilet, in a rudimentary form, has been invented by this point. It isn't in widespread use. A couple of more cholera outbreaks and it will be."

"Okay, if you will excuse me, I have to go visit the little house out back." Myers walked out the door and down the stairs. A cold wind blew as he stepped out the back of the building. He pulled his coat around himself. The building was made of wood and as he opened the door, he saw an old bench seat with one hole in it. *Now I have to worry about splinters and things freezing.* He sighed heavily. *I don't want to get stuck here. I want to go back to my own time.*

Chapter Twenty-Two

A chill January wind blew through the city as Dalton and Myers walked down to the river the next morning. No kids were playing anywhere near the promenade. As they walked to the café, they noticed that it had no windows that faced the river. They looked for an alternate location, but none would work.

The major let out a large sigh and said, "I guess we walk up and down the promenade for a few days."
"Isn't it going to look odd, two newcomers just show up out of nowhere and are suddenly here every day?"

"Maybe, but I doubt anyone will call the cops on a couple of men walking up and down the promenade."

"I suppose you're right. I should have brought my walking shoes."

Dalton was irritated, "You don't get it, do you? Your walking shoes are not era specific."

"I was just joking. I do think we should start out eating breakfast. It's easy to see that there are no children around this morning anyway."

"Kids aren't all that predictable. We still need to be close by, just in case."
"Sure, the café by the theater is as close as we can get, I think."

As the two sat down the server came out and gave them the menus. Myers ordered wiener schnitzel and Dalton asked for the bratwurst.

Myers was surprised when his food arrived. "This isn't a hot dog."

"You're German, and you don't know what wiener schnitzel is? It's breaded veal."

"I'm an American."

The server came back to the table. "Is everything fine?"

"No, everything is good," Dalton replied.

As she left, he lowered his voice. "I am completely disappointed in your mission preparation, Captain, and if we make it back alive, this will go on the report."

Looking like he had just been slapped, Myers mumbled, "Yes, Sir." He picked up his fork and ate.

Dalton knew he had been too hard on the younger officer, but he was feeling stressed, wondering if he had missed the correct day. Fuel would be an issue if they kept having to go back in time over and again. He didn't like the mission and hated to have to keep explaining things to Myers that were in the report he should have read.

When they were finished, they paid their tab and walked down by the river. There were no kids playing.

They had not said a word to each other since the restaurant. Myers broke the silence. "I'm sorry, Sir, for my lack of mission preparation."

"Let's get this mission done with and get home. Nothing else matters to me right now, and don't call me sir."

"Of course."

They walked up and down the promenade in the cold for the next few hours, but no children were playing. When dusk came, they walked back up to the hotel to get a good night's sleep. It was the same story the next day.

After two days, Myers asked, "Are we going back in time to a few days earlier?"

"Not yet. I'm going to give it one more day, then we'll go back to the first day of the month and stay here the whole of January, until we find the kids." They were doing their daily walk up and down the promenade when they passed a young man going the other way.

"That's him, Sir. That was Johann Kuehberger. I recognize him from the photo."

"We need to follow him, see where he goes." They both turned and followed the young boy. Soon they came upon a group of kids, playing by the water.

"What are they playing?" Myers asked.

"Cowboys and Indians."

The two men edged as close to the group as they could. One boy was chasing the young Hitler. Hitler was looking back as he ran, and fell into the river. Johann lunged for him. Grabbing Johann's arm and pulling him back, Myers yelled, "You'll drown, don't go in the water."

"I can save him."

Dalton ran to the water's edge. "I'll save him." He watched the young, panicked boy struggle. The four-year-old's eyes were full of fear as he thrashed in the river. Even though Hitler was within easy reach, at first, Dalton let him drift downriver in the icy water.

"I can't reach him," Dalton screamed.

Other rescuers had come to the shoreline. One jumped in, but Hitler had disappeared below the surface.

People were screaming, others were running. From around the bend in the river, a boat was launched, but efforts to find the boy were futile.

Dalton used the confusion to make his escape. He motioned to Myers that it was time to leave. The two men started walking back towards the hotel.

"It was awful, just awful. What have we done? We let a little boy die." Myers moaned.

"I'll never get the look of those innocent eyes out of my head. He was pleading for me to save him, but I was a false hope. No, I betrayed him. He knew I could reach him as he struggled in the water, but I didn't." Dalton shuddered at the thought.

Chapter Twenty-Three

The two of them checked out of the hotel quickly and then made their way towards the airplane. As they crossed the bridge they could see several boats in the river still searching for the young boy. Shouts erupted when they found the body and dragged it to shore. Dalton's stomach was knotted, still seeing the panic in Hitler's eyes. *He's going to grow up to be a monster.* He tried to reassure himself. *I'm already a monster.* He was nauseous, but didn't want to let on to Myers that he was weak.

After the bridge, they walked over and picked up their bikes. Pedaling fast to get out of town, they headed into the forest. The plane was still there and nobody had messed with it. They were both relieved, breaking down the bikes, they removed the camouflage. Stowing both into the plane, they didn't wait until nightfall, but started up the engines and lifted off.

Dalton could see people down below, looking at them, but they would be the size of an ant by that point. It didn't matter, he had killed a boy. All he wanted to do was return to his own time and forget what happened.

He pushed the stick forward. The plane gained speed. "Activate the Vmax drive," he ordered.

"Yes, Sir."

The engine hummed to life and Dalton could feel the g-forces pushing him back into the seat as the plane accelerated faster. As they flew, Dalton tried to raise the airbase. "Wolf to Erding, Wolf to Erding, come in please."

He called again, but there was no answer. "That's strange."

Suddenly sirens wailed in the cockpit and warning lights flashed. "Missile launch." Myers' high pitched voice called out.

"Get us out of here," Dalton ordered. He could see Myers engaging the Vmax drive. He checked his radar. "Two bogeys, three o'clock." The radar blips were moving nearer.

The drive came to life and the plane lurched forward.

Dalton put it in a steep dive as soon as the Vmax drive shut off. He found a sparsely populated forested area and put the plane down.

Without talking, the two men jumped out and put the camouflage over the plane, then ducked under the netting and pulled out their guns.

"Two turn of the century revolvers against modern rifles. This isn't going to be a fair fight. What does your intuition tell you about our chances of surviving this?" Myers asked.

"I don't know about you, but I'm planning on living."

The sound of a distant helicopter put the men on edge. "I guess we'll find out soon if you're right."

"We have only twelve shots between us. Only shoot if they're closing in on us."

"Yes, Sir."

The shadow of the aircraft came over them, but it didn't change its speed or flight path. Just as the men breathed a sigh of relief, another one came into view.

"They know we're down here. If they land troops, it'll be all over." Dalton swallowed hard.

"Two red stars on the side. That can't be good."

"No, it isn't. Reminds me of the old Soviet Union helicopters. They were the same style, but had a different insignia."

"What if we fire up the plane and make a run for it?"

Dalton fidgeted, "Not with them this close. We wouldn't stand a chance. Besides, I want to find out what's happening."

Myers ducked as yet another chopper passed nearby. "Yes, Sir."

It was two hours later when the flyovers finally stopped. The two men laid down to rest, their nerves were completely shot. Thinking that sleeping wasn't such a good idea after all, Dalton sat up. "I'll take the first watch. You get some shut-eye."

Myers didn't argue, just closed his eyes.

Three hours later, Dalton was shaking him awake. "Shhh, someone is coming and you're snoring."

"Sorry, Sir." He sat up and grabbed his gun.

"Let's not use that unless we have to. We need to get away from the plane, so whoever is coming won't spot it."

Myers complied and the two of them moved through the trees several yards.

A teenage girl was walking in the woods, she was wearing a sun dress and had long blonde hair. Whistling as she walked, she didn't notice the men at first. She stopped dead in her tracks when she did.

"Good afternoon," Myers tried to sound nonchalant.

"What are you doing here?" She eyed them suspiciously.

"We're lost, we are trying to find our way to town, maybe even the library."

Turning she pointed, "It's that way. Several kilometers. This is my father's co-op land, nobody is supposed to be in here. The government will be very upset."

"Oh, we don't want that. We will leave at once. Can you show us the way out?"

She hesitated for a moment, then relented. "Follow me."

They moved through the woods for a couple of miles before they came out into the open. A small village lay before them.

"There, in the center of town, next to the old church, is the library."

"Thank you very much," Myers replied.

Dalton nodded. The two men walked quickly away.

Chapter Twenty-Four

The men didn't go straight into town, but veered off and found a grove of trees to hide in. They waited until sundown, and then walked towards the library.

Passing a road sign, Dalton said, "That's interesting, it's in Russian and German."

"Troubling, you mean. Did Russia take over Germany? What have we done?"

"We've increased the enemies of the United States, looks like, if the U.S. still exists. Maybe Hitler wasn't so bad after all." He shuddered at the thought of the drowning four-year-old, still etched in his mind.

"What are we doing at the library?"

"Stealing a history book, so we know what's going on."
"So we're adding burglary to our list of crimes, along with murder."

"Yes."

There were few people on the street late at night. A couple came out of a bar and nearly ran in to the two men. The man looked Dalton and Myers up and down. Their 19th century clothes were out of place. Myers nodded at the man and walked past. As they approached the library, Dalton looked around to make sure no one was watching. He tried the door. It was locked.

"What now?" Myers said. He scanned the empty streets.

With a swift kick, the door burst open. The sound echoing through the town, Dalton ran inside.

It seemed like forever, but Dalton finally came out, carrying two books. "They don't use the Dewey decimal system here."

"Why would they? Let's get out of here. I hear someone coming."

As Dalton looked, two men were approaching.

Dalton and Myers ran the other direction and hid in someone's back yard.

Peeking around the corner, Dalton could see the library was now lit up. "We need to get further away. They're onto us."

"Yes, Sir."

Sneaking through back alleys and side streets, they made their way out of town. Then someone yelled out. "There they are."

Several men were running towards them. Myers fired one shot in the air and the men stopped.

"Don't waist ammo," Dalton snapped.

Now leading, Myers ran around corners and down cobblestone streets. They made their way out of town. He led them back to the grove of trees where they had hidden earlier. When they looked back at the town, it looked like someone had kicked over an anthill. There were men with flashlights everywhere, searching up and down every road.

"We should keep going, Sir. They might find us here."

"No, I think we're safe for now. They seem to think we're still in town."

"Yes, Sir," Myers replied, but his voice didn't sound confident.

Dawn came hours later. The two of them hadn't been spotted. There were only a few houses this far out, and the commotion in town had died down. They made their way to the forest where the plane was hidden. Checking it, Dalton was relieved that nothing had been touched.

As Myers stood guard, Dalton started to read the book to see what changes to history they had caused.

Two hours later, he joined Myers at lookout. "I found it. I know what happened. On September 14, 1930, according to our timeline, Hitler secured 107 seats in the Reichstag. The communists won 77. In the timeline this book is written in, the communists gained control of the Reichstag because there was no Hitler to oppose them. In September of 1939, Germany's invasion of Poland was to unite the two communist countries of Germany and Russia."

Dalton turned the page. "France did nothing, fearing an attack by the combined Russia and German armies. A year later, France held their own elections and the communists of that country received ten percent of the vote. A larger political party attacked the communists and Germany invaded on the pretense that their followers were getting persecuted. A week later, Russia joined in and the French were in full retreat. The whole European continent is now communist, except for England and Sweden. Sweden is neutral and England has made a separate peace with the German-Russian alliance after several years at war.

"North and South America are the only holdouts. An invasion was attempted, but the U.S. was able to turn it back, mid-Atlantic with the first atomic bomb.

"The Empire of Japan is still alive and kicking. They have had several armed conflicts with the Russians. All have ended in a stalemate, but the threat of another one ties down a lot of troops."

Myers swallowed hard. "So we did the wrong thing?"

"Yes, the Jews are getting persecuted still, by the Russians and the Germans. The war has never stopped. There is always fighting between one faction or another. Africa is a major battleground with the major powers trying to divide up the territories. More people die in this timeline than the other one. We need to go back to Passau."

Chapter Twenty-Five

Both men's attention was diverted to a cracking branch. As they looked, they saw the young girl they had encountered the day before leading three police officers towards them.

"Sir, go get the plane started, I will hold them off."

Dalton didn't hesitate, but ran to the plane and pulled off the camouflage netting. There was no time to stow it. He left it on the ground, around the plane.

Myers held his fire until the plane engine hummed to life. The policemen were now running towards the sound. He fired at them to slow them down. Three shots rang out and one of the officers went down. The other two dragged their wounded comrade behind some trees.

Dalton heard a helicopter overhead. He motioned for Myers to come. As he looked up, he saw soldiers rappelling out of the chopper. Dalton fired several shots from his revolver, out of the cockpit. The soldiers ducked, but only momentarily. As soon as they had taken cover, they were returning fire. Myers was almost to the plane, when something knocked him over. He stood up again and climbed into his seat.

There were thuds against the side of the airplane. Dalton wasted no time in getting airborne. As soon as they were in the sky, he saw three enemy jets heading towards him.

"Get us out of here, and I *mean now*," Dalton yelled.

The Vmax engine came to life, buffeted sharply as they headed back in time.

Dalton checked again. The other planes had disappeared from radar. He let out the breath he'd been holding. "That was a near thing."

There was no response. "Myers, are you okay?"

Still silence.

"Myers?"

The plane stopped buffeting and he could see the city of Passau beneath him. He headed for the same woods they were at before. Ignoring the extra noise caused by a quick landing, he brought the plane down, then immediately jumped out. Myers was slumped in his seat. He checked for a pulse but there wasn't one.

Dalton dropped to the ground and put his head in his hands. *Why, why, why? It's such a stupid mission. Idiots, they're all idiots.*

He sat there for an hour. Nobody approached the plane. He wouldn't have cared if they had. It had been all a big mistake, and now Myers was dead.

Heaving a large sigh, he climbed back up on to the plane and pulled the body out. Digging a shallow hole with a makeshift shovel, from a faring panel, he placed the body into it. He packaged up the books and most of the money he had brought with him in a waterproof bag and then buried them too. He stuffed the rest of the cash in his pocket.

"Ashes to ashes, dust to dust." He couldn't remember the rest.

He looked down at Myers. *I wouldn't have mentioned your lack of preparation in my report. Honestly, I wouldn't have.*

He pulled Myers' dog tag off and then piled rocks up on the body. It was all a waste.

He sat there until night fell, then he realized he had no idea what day it was. He pulled the bike out of the airplane and assembled it, then rode it in to town, hoping it wasn't too late to check into a hotel.

Arriving in town, Dalton was relieved to see the place they had stayed before had the lights on. He walked in. "I would like a room, oh, and what day is it?"

The older woman behind the desk smiled. "Have you been traveling a long time?"

"Yes, a very long time."

"It is January 6th."

"Thank you so much." *The day before, he put me here the day before.* He felt so relieved. He imagined the dying Myers setting the controls. It would be the last thing he did before he passed out.

"Your key." The lady's voice brought him back from his thoughts.

"Thank you."

"You have no luggage?"

"No, I travel light."

She smiled, "Have a good night."

He walked upstairs to the same room they had before. Sitting on the bed, he realized he hadn't had any sleep for two days. It had been so stressful. He laid down, not bothering to take off his clothes, and fell asleep.

Chapter Twenty-Six

The crisp cold air of January stung his cheeks as Major Dalton made his way to the promenade that ran along the river. He knew what time he had to be there and the best place to sit for the drama that was about to unfold. When the young Hitler fell into the water, he was determined to save him, but his intervention wasn't necessary. Johann Kuehberger pulled the four-year-old out of the icy waters of the Inn River. The young boy shivered as people who had been walking by went down to the water's edge to help. Someone put their coat over him as they led him home to his parents' house. Dalton still had a flashback of the panicking eyes of a young boy about to drown. This made amends for his earlier murder.

His mission complete, the Major made his way back to the airplane. The pile of rocks that held the body of Captain Myers drew his attention. *I can't leave him here.*

He un-piled the rocks, threw Myers over his shoulder and struggled, carrying the body back up into the cockpit. The captain's seat was still covered in blood. He dropped the body in it, then strapped it down into the seat.

It was an exhausting effort. He set the controls on the Vmax to bring the plane back to the 21st Century. On the way back down the side of the airplane, he noticed the bullet holes with oil coming out of them. "No," he exclaimed. His heart sank. The oil tanks that had been moved to the side to allow room for storage had made the plane vulnerable to small arms fire. Several bullets had hit it. "No," he moaned again. He put his flight suit over the period clothes, not knowing where he would end up when the plane went down. He didn't have enough gas to get back to America, but if he could get back to his own time, he could figure out a way to get home.

Knowing that he didn't have a choice, he would either have to fly the airplane out of there, or destroy it. Technology like that didn't belong in the 1890s. He climbed into the cockpit and fired up the engine. To his relief, it started.

He took off from the forest, gaining altitude until he was clear, then he throttled the plane forward. He had to reach back behind him, to where Meyers was, to switch on the Vmax drive. It pushed the plane faster, but only for a few seconds. The drive began to smoke badly, then shut off.

It was still smoking as he rocketed across the sky, but nothing he could do would turn the drive back on again. It was frozen. Turning his plane to the west, all he could do was to fly as far as he could, then crash the plane, to destroy it.

As he flew over Germany and France, he realized that only the Vmax drive had been damaged. It had had enough oil to jump back in time to save Hitler, but as he did so, the rest of the oil dripped out. Turning it back on afterwards was the end of it.

There was no hope, in his mind, of making the parts to fix it. Many of the processes to do so hadn't been invented.

The plane started to sputter. He put it in a slight dive. He was out over the Atlantic, trying to reach the American shore. He wasn't going to make it. Shuddering, the engine died completely. He held the stick in both hands and would glide it as far as he could, but the weight of the plane was too great and it started in a steep dive. Not wanting it to go into a spin before he could get out, Dalton ejected.

A parachute would seem strange to the people of this century, but still might draw the attention of potential rescuers.

He hit the water hard, jarring his back and causing him to groan out loud. He turned just in time to watch the plane splash down. Dusk had settled in, and he could see the lights of a ship in the distance, so he fired his only flare. His heart raced as he watched the ship alter course and head towards him.

Chapter Twenty-Seven

The German captain of the steamship looked up and down at Dalton, who was standing in front of him in the cluttered office. "Where did you say you came from again?"

"From the ship, *Ugly Duckling*. It sank right before you arrived. There were only two of us left. The other man went down with the ship." Dalton had managed to slip off his life vest and flight suit while in the water, leaving his period specific clothes.

"How many tons was she?"

"Small, a hundred tons is all." Dalton was guessing. He wasn't a navy man.

"That is small, crew should be about ten men. What has happened to the others?"

"Ship started to sink, they left in a life boat. The two of us were to follow, but our boat leaked so badly, we made our way back to the ship and tried to pump her out. It was no use. She sank. I was able to get away, but Myers was caught in the rigging and went down with the ship."

"Should I look for the survivors? Are they nearby?"

Dalton swallowed hard. He didn't like lying, but the truth was unbelievable. "No, Sir. They left days ago. Should have been picked up by now."

"I'll put it out on the wireless, see if anyone has found them."

"Yes, Sir."

"Meanwhile, I don't know what to do with you." The captain scratched his head. "I know, I need another stoker. I had one die on the way over. You can take his place. You can earn the rest of your passage to America. If you want to join the crew, after that, you should be able to. Depending on how much work I can get out of you. You look soft to me."

Dalton's heart sank. It was a brutal job, one that he wasn't going to like. "Yes, Sir," he mumbled.

Escorting Dalton out of the office, the first officer made his way below deck, to the chief engineer. "You have a new stoker. His name is Robert Dalton. He's the man we plucked from the sea."

The engineer looked Dalton up and down, just as the captain had done previously. He looked a little doubtful, but nodded. "Yes, Sir. I will put him to work right away."

When Dalton entered the engine room, he thought the boilers looked like fire spewing dragons. Each boiler had three doors with fire shining through the windows. A group of men stood in front of the doors and every time one opened, shovelfuls of coal were tossed in.

"Take your shirt off. You don't want it catching fire."

Dalton did as he was told.

The engineer handed him a shovel. "Follow their lead. It won't take long to figure it out."

Dalton walked over to the group. Right as he did one of the doors opened and the flames leapt out. The intense heat increased. He began to shovel like the other men. His skin reddened.

"Drink," one of the men demanded, handing him a bottle. He took a long swig. To his surprise, it was wine, good wine.

Another man threw water on him. "Your hair was starting to steam. It's a bad sign."

"Thanks," Dalton replied.

Another door opened and the process was repeated, again and again, over the next four hours.

Then, at last, more men came down the ladders and replaced them and the tired men, black with coal dust, climbed out of the engine room and out onto the deck.

"You did well for your first day. The next morning will be the worst. As you wake, your aching muscles will scream with pain. It gets better after a week or two. The name's Wilhelm."

"Robert. Thank you for your help."

The men made their way out onto the open deck, where buckets of water waited for them. Each, in near unison, dumped it over his head, in a vain attempt to get the dirt and grime of the coal off their skins. Dalton followed suit.

"This way, Robert. Now we eat. They feed us well."

Dalton followed his new friend to the crew's mess. They sat down in front of boiled potatoes, butter, with some type of meat, he wasn't sure what. It all tasted good. He thought about asking what year it was, but didn't know how to do that without looking stupid. "Where are we heading?" It was something he wouldn't be expected to know, having just been plucked from the sea.

"New York City. We'll be there in three days. They always give the engineering crew liberty, while the rest of the crew stays with the ship. I can show you some fun places, if you know what I mean."

Dalton smiled and nodded. It meant that it was just before or just after world war one, or the Great War, as they would refer to it at the time. "When was this ship built?"

"1893."

"So how old is it? My math isn't too good."

"Six years old."

Dalton smiled. He made a fool of himself, but not a big fool. *1899, I only came forward five years before the Vmax drive cut out.* Now to try and find out where the plane was.

"How fast are we going?"

"Captain likes to maintain fifteen knots."

"Thanks."

Chapter Twenty-Eight

His muscles screamed with pain as Wilhelm shook him awake. "It's time."

Dalton rolled out of his bunk and onto the floor. It took all of his effort to stand up and fight the stiffness by moving.

"Come, Robert." Wilhelm beckoned.

"Coming." Dalton followed him to the boilers.

"You will feel better when you start shoveling. Get those muscles warm, but you will pay dearly for it again in the morning. Only two more days until we are in the Gotham. Then I will show you some fun that you will never write home about."

Two more days. Just two more days, Dalton thought. The door opened and the flames shot out. He shoveled the coal in.

The four hour shift went painfully slow. Several times he had to dunk his head into a bucket full of water, but even that didn't cool him down very much. The room was hot, the water was hot, and it was even more unbearable when the boiler doors opened. Flames leapt out, licking at their bare chests.

Finally it was over. The new crew arrived to begin their arduous task and his group clambered up the steps to an awaiting meal. After eating, Dalton and Wilhelm sat out on the deck. It was a cloudless day and they watched as the sea raced by.

"So, where are you from, Robert?"

"Boston."

Wilhelm sat up and stared at him. "You are an American? I thought you were German."

"My mother, she was German. She taught me how to speak it."

"All this time I thought you were from Bremen, like most of the rest of us."

"I was born in Germany, but live in Boston. Don't tell the others."

"Why not?"

"Not all Germans like Americans. Things will become worse between us in the future."

"I don't know of anyone on the crew who hates Americans, but your secret is safe with me." He paused for a moment. "What about the future?"

Dalton swallowed hard. "There is so much tension in Europe. I think the United States will get dragged into a conflict over there. How can we not? We may not be on Germany's side. There are strong ties to England over here. I mean, if it comes to that."

Wilhelm sat back. "I just don't see another war. People are beyond that. I think they are a thing of the past."

"I hope you're right." Dalton grimaced inside. Knowing the horrific future of wars turned his stomach. As he sat up, he moaned a little. His muscles were tightening up again.

"One more shift, Robert. We sail into the harbor the next morning, before we are scheduled to work."

"I don't know how you do it."

"It's a way of life now. The body gets used to it. I started young, not like you."

"I'm not that old."

"To start as a stoker, you are."

"I suppose you're right." Dalton stretched his sore muscles.

"We need to get some sleep, morning comes early."

"Yes, it does."

As he started for his bunk, the chief engineer stopped him. "Captain wishes to see you."

"Yes, Sir."

When he arrived at the captain's quarters, the man was sitting behind his desk, drumming his fingers.

"You wanted to see me, Sir?"

"There is no ship named the *Ugly Duckling*. No one has seen anyone in a life boat anywhere near the water." The tone was accusatory.

Dalton stood tall. "There was an *Ugly Duckling*. It wasn't named that, but it was my name for it. It sank right before you arrived. I came from Germany on it, but it didn't make it. There was no other crew, just my friend and me. It was a stupid thing to try to make it that far, but worth the try, I thought. My friend's dead, and I am a stoker on a ship unfamiliar to me."

The captain just grunted and then motioned him to go away. Dalton didn't waste any time doing so.

The Major tossed and turn on the straw filled mattress. He had been so tired the first night, he barely noticed it, but tonight was different. The straw poked him as he turned over. Wishing he had some pain medicine and a real bed, it was the first time he reflected on his circumstances. He was stuck in the past like he thought he would be. He had tried to avoid it, but going back to save Hitler had sealed his fate. Myers' death was the worst of it. He hadn't expected that. He had hoped that the Captain would have made it back to their own time. Depression hit him. The feeling of hopelessness was like a sledge hammer, stopping his restless spirit. He fell into a dreamless sleep.

Chapter Twenty-Nine

"Robert, we are here. New York City." Wilhelm shook Dalton until he opened his eyes. "Come see."

Fatigue gave way to enthusiasm and soon the two of them were standing on the deck, watching as the ship sailed into the harbor.

He looked for the iconic Empire State Building, but then realized it wasn't built yet. The Brooklyn Bridge was though. He admired it. It looked fresh, almost new, unlike the bridge he had passed over many times. He found it interesting that most of the traffic across the bridge was horse drawn. He was indeed in a different time. A pang of sadness passed over him.

"Isn't it wonderful, Robert? The world's most modern city."

"Yes, it is something, isn't it?"

"I can't wait to show you all the places you don't tell your mother about."

Dalton let out a heavy sigh. "I won't be coming back to the ship. I'm going to try to make a new life here in the city."

Wilhelm turned. "You're leaving? Not that I blame you. A stoker's job is not a good one for someone your age, but I thought you might at least have fun with me in the city first."

The ship slowed down and started its turn into the dock.

"No, those places you speak of are for young men. I must try and find my way in the world."

"Good luck to you, Robert. I will give you my address in Germany. You write me when you get settled."

"I'll do that."

The two men shook hands, then Dalton made his way back to his bunk. His pants were ruined, but his shirt was fairly fresh, as he hadn't worn it much. It was still crusted with salt water, though.

He thought of Colonel Ross. He would be making the best of things. Unlike Dalton, he would be relishing in living history and loving every second of it. *I should be more like Ros*s, he thought. That was the way to get through this.

Washing his pants out in the sink, he put them on wet. As he turned, the chief engineer was standing there. "Here's your pay. You did good, for an old man. I have a spot for you, if you want to make the return journey."

"No, America is my home. I'll be staying."

"As you wish. Good luck to you."

"Thanks."

When he arrived back on the deck, the ship had tied up and the gang plank was lowered. Dalton stepped off the ship.

A morning breeze blew off the water as he walked away from the ship. He wouldn't miss it, although he would miss Wilhelm. The city was alive with longshoremen offloading and loading in the busy port. Two blocks away from the dock, it had business men going from one building to another. A few blocks later, he saw children playing in the streets.

That was where he wanted to live, a place that was young and vibrant. He talked to several people and found a room to rent, with a small kitchen. The bed was much softer than the one on the ship. The room was very bare otherwise with old, stained wall paper. The bathroom was down the hall. He went back in the city and found a place to buy a pair of pants and two shirts. That would be all he needed for now.

His money wasn't going to last long, so he looked for work. He knew he didn't want a manual labor job like the last one he had. He found a brokerage firm that was hiring. Stocks were up and the country was in a prosperous time, so brokerage firms were adding personnel.

Dalton walked into the building. The secretary was a redhead with light freckles on the bridge of her nose. She seemed very nice, but shy. She told him that the manager was only looking for men with experience. Dalton asked her to try and see if the manager would make an exception. He wouldn't, so Robert talked to her for a few minutes.

Every day he would bring the secretary a flower and ask her to try again. After trying to get an interview for two weeks, the manager finally decided to talk to him.

"You're only here because you're the most persistent man I have ever met."

Dalton smiled. "Thank you for agreeing to see me."

"Not my doing, my secretary has taken a liking to you, after all your visits. She's the one who talked me into it. So what makes you think you'd be a good broker?"

"I was a major in the military. I have intimate knowledge of several upcoming projects. A few dollars in the right stocks will put a lot of money in your pockets." He didn't know what the insider trading laws were at this time, but he guessed there weren't any.

Ted, the manager, was almost drooling at the thought. His brown eyes brightened as he smiled. "You're hired."

Chapter Thirty

His office was barely bigger than a broom closet. It had a candlestick style telephone on a small desk, and a note pad with two fountain pens. The secretary did all the typing for the five stock brokers of the firm. The typewriter was a massive thing with the keys on the bottom and the letters on arms, forming a semicircle just above that. It had a roller mechanism on the top.

He sat down with the pen and paper and plotted out the upcoming history of the United States, as he could remember it. The pen made a mess on his paper as he had never used a fountain pen before. He had to stop and clean up several times. Not used to having to let the ink dry before he moved his hand across the paper, he had ink all over.

The boss came in as he was wiping up again.

"That's the messiest paper I've seen in a long time."

"Having problems with the pen."

"I'll have Mary bring you another one. I can't have my newest employee making a mess. I'll get you today's numbers and tomorrow you'll be out on the floor."

Dalton swallowed hard. *The floor of the New York Stock Exchange*? He was sure he wasn't ready for that.

He went to the wash room and cleaned up. He was glad to see the building had indoor plumbing. The tank to the toilet was almost at ceiling level and the seat near the ground. The sink had a hand pump and a basin to collect the water.

When he arrived back at his desk, Mary, the secretary, was waiting for him. Her hair was pulled up loosely around her head, and there was another twist above that. It looked like a hat made of hair. Her eyes were a light blue, and her lips red. When she smiled, she showed her bright white teeth. "Here is a new pen. They leak sometimes."

"And sometimes the user makes a mess because he's not used to working with one," he joked.

She let out a slight giggle, like a shy school girl. She even seemed to blush a little.

"Thank you for the pen. I will try and be more careful than I was the last time," he added.

She smiled, then went back to her typing. He looked for a ring on her left hand, but there wasn't one. When he sat back down, he threw the paper away and started over. This time he would let the ink dry with every line to avoid smearing. The writing was still blotchy, but not smeared as it was the time before. When he finished, he blew on the paper to finish drying it. He had listed all the major events on it that he could remember, assassinations, wars, elections, earthquakes, and disasters. That took him to the 1960s. He figured he wouldn't live past then. He put the paper in his desk drawer and left for the day.

Ted walked into Dalton's office. He was highly suspicious of the new man. His rivals had sent people over to try and find out what was going on in Ted's office. He was making more money than any of them and they wanted to know why. Ted picked up the paper from the trash and looked at it. It was messy, but he could make out dates and events. *Who is this guy?* He wondered. *Does he have a crystal ball?*

He took the paper and stuck it in his file cabinet. It could prove very interesting.

Dalton arrived at his apartment. The neighbors were arguing about money, he could easily hear them through the thin walls. He tried to rest, but it was no use. Soon the door slammed and the man stomped out. After an hour, he heard a radio turn on. *That's what I need, something to listen to.* He decided then and there to buy one with his first pay check. His cook stove was a one-burner, and he only had the one pot. It was left over by the previous tenant and was in poor shape. It was better than nothing. He boiled some water then put some vegetables in it. The ones he had picked up at the market on the way home. He had no ice box. He had no way of preserving food, so he would have to buy fresh every day. The stove was coal fired and hard to light, but he managed somehow.

The soup needed salt. He vowed to buy some next time he was out. The bed was stuffed with cotton and a lot more comfortable than the straw stuffed one he had on the ship. Still, he looked around the sparse apartment and thought of what he had lost. The cell phone was the hardest to take. He had been on his constantly. He would check the weather and get caught up on the news, then check on his poor old mother. *Mother.* The thought of his mother, grieving his loss, saddened him. *She must think I'm dead.* It was his lowest moment of the whole ordeal. At least in Passau, he had hope of making it back to his own time. Now the time machine was on the bottom of the ocean and he was stuck. He sat there, wishing he had something to drink. He counted his money. No chance to buy liquor on what he had left.

Chapter Thirty-One

Dalton had never seen such pandemonium. Prices were yelled out and trades were made. He stood next to his boss, who was making deals right and left. He had been given a list of stocks to buy and sell by the secretary. He was fulfilling those orders.

Each deal was written down by both parties. The trading continued until four in the afternoon and there were no breaks in between, not even for lunch. He had to eat his sandwich while trading. At the end of the day, arrangements were made to exchange the stocks and in a day or two, they would be hand delivered to the customers. mostly banks and financial institutions.

Dalton had a headache when he arrived back in the office. Mary smiled as he and Ted entered. He handed his notes to her and she started typing them out.

"What did you think? Busy, huh?" Ted asked.

"Yes, and fast paced."

"You'll be up to speed in no time. I'll let you do the trading tomorrow, but I'll be by your elbow the rest of the week. With your insights of upcoming military contracts, our customers will be rich."

"How about us? When do we get rich?"

Ted did a double take. "Us? We get rich by making them rich."

"You don't invest in the market yourself?"

Ted let out a large sigh. "I've seen so many fortunes lost in the market, I keep my money safely stashed in my pocket."

With a nervous laugh, Robert replied, "I hear what you're saying, but I want to invest. I want to make money and move out to the Hamptons."

"Where?"

"East end of Long Island." A chill went down Dalton's back. Had he blown it? He didn't know when the Hamptons became a place to be.

"Oh, that's mostly potato farms, as far as I know. I guess there are a few villages up there. Why would anyone want to live there?"

"I've been there before. A nice house off the beach would make a wonderful summer home. It's a chance to get out of the city once in a while."

"Not for me."

Ted grabbed his jacket off the hook. "I'm going home. Have a good weekend."

They were both standing next to Mary's desk by that point. When Ted left, Robert went back to get his things. When he turned around, Mary was standing in his doorway.

"Sorry, I couldn't help but overhear you. It's a small office. Ted doesn't know anything. I spent a week at the East End last summer. It's a wonderful place, with beautiful beaches. Who wouldn't want to live there?"

"Thank you for that. I thought I was losing my mind."

Mary's smile disappeared. "Why would you do that?"

Dalton was in stunned silence for a second. "Um, it's just a saying."

"I've never heard that before. What does it mean?"

"I've never really thought about it. I guess it means I was thinking the Hamptons would be a nice place to live, but Ted was trying to convince me otherwise."

She stood there for a minute, contemplating, then announced, "I still don't understand."

"Let it go. I'll try to never use it again. Say, do you want to go get a cup of coffee somewhere?"

She turned, put her hands on her hips, "Why, I never."

"I'm sorry, I did that wrong. What should I have said?"

"That is just not a way to talk to a young lady. You ask if you can come calling. My mother warned me about men like you."

"I'm not like that, really I'm not."

She folded her arms. "I don't know, you use words and expressions I've never heard before, and you are very forward and improper. I must be going." She left in a huff.

Come calling? I wonder what that means. He shook his head as he left the office. *What words do I use that she's never heard before? How was I supposed to know the*

Hamptons isn't a popular place yet? He kicked himself. He knew all the right words to use for 1894 Germany, but he didn't have the same list for America. He felt so lost and lonely. *Can't a guy just ask a girl out in this time and age?*

Back at his small apartment, he looked down at the street and watched the kids play. They were interrupted a few times, by horse drawn carts. The game would stop, the wagon would pass and they were playing in the middle of the street again. He fired up the stove and cooked some meat he had purchased at the butchers on his way home. *Everything's harder,* he complained to himself. He couldn't let himself get depressed though. He might never get over it. His circumstances were not going to change anytime soon.

Chapter Thirty-Two

On Saturday morning, Robert walked down the street on his way to the market. He passed a bookstore he hadn't noticed before. It was closed, but it gave him an idea. He walked up to a merchant in the market and asked, "Is there a library around here?"

"The Astor Library."

"How do I get there?"

"You take Broadway to Fourth and turn right. Then go to Lafayette and turn left. The library will be on your right. Don't go today. It won't be open."

"Thank you very much."

Dalton finished his shopping and went back to his apartment. He bought food for two days as he figured the market wouldn't be open on Sunday. Today he would eat fresh fruit. He didn't feel like cooking. He sat down, wishing he had a book or two. Monday, he would definitely buy one, or go to the library, even though it was very far away.

He couldn't stand being in his apartment one more minute, so he wandered around the streets until he found a park. He walked through the park for a while and then he found a bench to sit on. There he observed the people around him. The men tipped their hats as they passed people. No words were exchanged, just a gentle nod.

The women would respond by nodding back. There were children, but they seemed to be in their own world of play, ignoring the goings-on of the adults.

He would listen to conversations when in earshot of passersby. They talked differently than he did. He would listen to the speech patterns so he could get them right.

Dalton mused how prepared he had been when he traveled to 1894 Passau, but now he was totally unprepared. He couldn't even speak his own language in America, as well as he spoke 1800s German.

Treating himself to dinner, he ate at the café on the corner instead of firing up his stove. The weather was warming, and his apartment was stuffy. He was surprised at how little it cost. Still worrying about running out of money before his first payday, he decided he would not eat out again until he had the check in his hand.

When Sunday came around, even though he wasn't a religious man, Dalton decided to go to church. He figured someone would ask what church he belonged to, and he needed an answer.

His mother had been Lutheran so he decided to attend that one. Walking around the streets the day before, he had come across one near the park. He waited outside during the morning until he saw the congregation entering the building and then followed them in. The building was a simple structure compared to the Catholic cathedrals in the area. It had a spire past the top of the building and then flattened out. It was built of brick and had a sharp pitch to the roof. When he entered, there was a feeling of calm in the room. The altar was at the far end and there were stained glass windows in the front of the building. Dalton made his way to one of the pews, only to be asked to move by the family who normally sat there.

"Where can I sit?" he asked.

"Back four rows are for visitors and new members."

He shrugged and moved back.

The preacher gave a rousing sermon on loving your fellow man. The choir was amazing, filling the room with music. When the service was over, he went to leave, but the pastor had made his way to the door and greeted the members of his flock as they left.

When it was Dalton's turn to shake his hand, the pastor said, "I've not seen you before. Are you visiting?"

"No, I've recently moved to the area."

"Good, very good. Will we be seeing more of you?"

"I believe you will."

"Good."

Dalton thought the man was going to ask his name, but he didn't want to delay the line any more so he moved on out the door. It was sunny outside and he enjoyed the walk home. When he arrived, he fired up the stove and cooked dinner.

Chapter Thirty-Three

Monday morning, Dalton woke up and ate some of the fruit he had bought on Saturday. He then made his way to work. Mary was cold to him as he passed her by, but he gave her a warm hello anyway. She said, "Hello," without bothering to look up. He made his way to his office and sat down.

Ted came in a few minutes later. "Well, it's your turn to be the trader today. Don't worry, I'll be at your shoulder the whole time. Here is the list of the stocks we want to keep an eye on. If there's a good price on them, we will buy."

"Sounds good, I'm ready." Dalton wasn't. He would fake it though, because this was his job.

He was a natural at it. His military training took over. He organized buys and sales and was able to think clearly despite everything that was happening around him. By the end of the day, he had made so many deals; it took an hour to write them up.

"Well, you don't seem to need me now, do you? You are on your own from now on." Ted smacked him on the back.

"But…"

"But, what? Are you sure you haven't done this before?"

"I haven't. I'm sure of it."

Ted smiled and the two of them headed back to the office. Mary was gone for the day. He sighed, but grabbed his things and headed down to the bookstore he had found.

When he arrived, the owner was locking the door.

"Please, Sir, I need a book."

The man turned to Dalton. "What are you in need of? If you're buying, I will open it back up."

"I need a book on etiquette."

The owner let out a hardy laugh. "Must be a woman involved, that's the only reason a man buys a book on etiquette. Come in, I guess the wife can wait supper a few minutes. I have just the book you need."

He unlocked the door and went in. He came back with a book. "The Gentlemen's Book of Etiquette and Manual of Politeness, by Cecil B. Hartley."

Dalton looked at it. "Yes, this looks like exactly what I need. Thank you very much."

"That will be fifty cents."

"Sure." Dalton replied as he handed over the coins. "Thanks again."

"You have a good day, Sir."

He went back to his small apartment and started reading. The light bulb came on when he got to the part about courting. So *that's what Mary was talking about. I had no idea.* There was a lot more to this calling than met the eye.

He knew how to do it now. Realizing how forward he must have seemed in this time, he knew he owed her an apology.

Continuing to trade stocks through the week, Ted left Dalton alone. When Friday came, it was time for his first payday. He was paid in cash, much to Dalton's surprise. It was good though, because he didn't have to get a bank account right away.

"My first payday was a fraction of what you made. You really are a natural at this, Robert. I'm glad I hired you. One day you must tell me what new military weapons are on the drawing board. I could trade in the companies that make those."

"We're just barely scratching the surface of what's about to happen. We're not talking army inventions either. Did you know there are plans in work to build a heavier-than-air craft that flies?"

"I've heard of such a thing, but I don't believe it."

"They will succeed, I'm sure of it."

"What makes you so sure?"

"I can feel it."

Ted smiled. "We'll see about that. I'll be trading in heavier-than-air craft stock soon."

"Not soon, in ten years maybe. Remember the name Curtis."

"I have to get home. You have a good day." Ted walked out the door after tipping his hat to Mary.

Dalton wanted to say something to her, but she didn't turn around. She left right after Ted did.

Locking up, Dalton headed home. He fired up his stove. Tonight, he wanted a warm meal, even though it meant heating up his apartment.

Chapter Thirty-Four

On his way to work the next morning, he arrived a little late because he stopped to by some flowers at the market. His book didn't cover such a purpose, but he anticipated the women of the age would love flowers as much as they did in the future.

Mary's eyes brightened as he handed them to her. "I'm sorry for being so forward before. I would like to ask your permission to call on you sometime."

"They're beautiful. Let me give you my address. I would love for you to come calling."

As she handed him the card, she said, "Ted is already at the stock exchange. He said to get down there as soon as possible."

"I'm on my way." He smiled as he left, stuffing the card in his shirt pocket.

The market was chaotic that day. Dalton started in right away, making more trades than he had the previous week. When the day was finally over, he arrived back at the office to find both Mary and Ted had headed home for the evening.

He pulled his list of historical events from his desk drawer. Boer War starting in October. It meant it was time to invest in steel. They needed steel to build rifles and cannons. Mauser and Krag-Jorgensen rifles would revolutionize warfare. Other nations, not involved in the conflict, would modernize their armories after the war. He lived modestly, so he had some money to invest. A little at a time, patience was the key. When the world changed, he would be a step ahead.

Shoving the paper back in the drawer, he headed home to another lonely night in his empty apartment. He touched his pocket to see if Mary's card was still there. It was. In a day or two he would call on her. She could make his banishment to the past bearable.

The next few days were busy in the markets. He took the time to trade for his own steel company stock. Just a few shares, but it didn't go unnoticed by Ted. At the office that night, Ted waited for him.

Dalton was surprised to see that Ted was still there when he opened the door.

"Have any new hot tips?" Ted's arms were folded.

"I'm just doing what you trained me to do."

"I heard you did some personal trades. Did you want to share your insights? I hired you because you were supposed to know things about army plans, but you haven't divulged any of those. What is it about U.S. Steel that causes you to invest in it?"

Dalton didn't know what to do. Ted's face was red. He had never seen him like this. "I thought it was a good investment."

"There's something else going on, isn't there? If I had a limited investment income, I would buy a whole lot of different things before I would ever think about buying steel. Then again, I'm not an ex-army guy."

"Fine, I can't tell you my sources, but war is brewing in Africa between the Boers and the English. There will be a lot of rifles and cannons sold before it's over. You can tell your clients about that."

"I can't risk their money on a war that may or may not happen."

"It will happen. I guarantee it, and it will have huge repercussions."

Ted's eyes widened. "You have a crystal ball or something?"

"Something like that."

"I'll tell my clients that tensions are brewing in Africa and war is on the horizon, but if you're wrong, it's your job."

"I'm not wrong." Dalton replied.

"I'm going home. See you Monday morning. Oh, and try to be on time." Ted picked up his hat and walked towards the door.

"I will."

Dalton locked up and made his way to the street. He pulled Mary's card out of his pocket. Today was the day. He read the address and walked in that direction. He took the street car, and then a train to Fordham, a rural area close to the city. Her family lived in a stately house there. When Dalton set eyes on it for the first time, he realized where the idea for the house he would later build in the Hamptons had come from.

Chapter Thirty-Five

Mary was all smiles as she came to the door. She was in a blue dress, trimmed in lots of lace, and her hair was let down in a ponytail that was tied with a bow. "Come in." she beckoned.

"Thank you so much. Nice house."

"It's Daddy's, I just live here." She led him into the parlor where there was a loveseat and two overstuffed chairs. She sat down in the middle of the loveseat with her full dress taking up most of the room on it. He sat down in a chair across from her.

She straightened out her dress while she smiled at him. "I only see you at work for a few minutes each day. I know so little about you."

"There isn't much to know really. I was born just outside of Woodstock, Vermont. Not the famous Woodstock."

"The famous Woodstock?"

He let out a nervous laugh, realizing what he had said. "I mean, there's another Woodstock in New York. It's more famous than my town."

"Oh, really? I've never heard of either of them."

"Yes, a lot of Woodstocks out there. Where were you born?"

"I was born here in New York. Been here all my life."

"That's nice. Done any traveling?"

"No, I have everything here I could ever want. Why would I need to go anywhere else?"

"There's a whole world out there."

"And you, do you travel much?"

"I've been all over the United States, and to Europe. Germany is especially beautiful. I was in the town of Passau not long ago. That is right on the Danube River."

She smiled. Her eyes brightened and he could tell he struck a chord with her. "The Danube, is it as romantic as they say?"

"More so."

"I read a book about it once. They say it's so tranquil the ships ride on it like it was a lake. Were you able to ride a riverboat up and down the river, or were you there on business?"

The picture of a young boy drowning flashed across his mind. Then he thought of Captain Myers, dead in the back seat of his plane. He shuddered at the thoughts.

"Is something wrong?" Her face was etched with concern.

"No, nothing. Only, I was with a friend, and he died near there. It just brought back memories. I'm sorry."

"How did he die?"

"He was mistaken for someone else and shot. He died shortly after. Let's not talk of him though, let's talk of the world. The west coast is beautiful, with cliffs that border the sea."

The moment had been lost. The sparkle was out of her eyes. "You were shot at too, weren't you?"

He looked in her eyes. There was sweetness in them, and sympathy.

"Yes, I was. It was a mission. I was in the military. We were to stop a disaster from happening, but we failed. I had to retreat, and he was killed. I tried to bring him home but I didn't make it. My ship went down in the middle of the Atlantic with his body in it. I was picked up by a passing German freighter. It was a bad time for me."

Mary's father walked into the parlor. She shifted nervously as he sat down, seeming uncomfortable with his presence. "An army man, eh? I overheard your conversation. I was in the army in my younger days. 36th New York. Fought at Chancellorsville."

Dalton's head reared back in shock. "You fought in the Civil War?"

"Yes, it was only thirty four years ago. I was a lad of seventeen at the time. There are a lot of us veterans still around, but we're a dying breed. Most of the officers of our unit have passed on. What unit were you in?"

"I was in a special service group. It didn't have a number. It was formed for one mission and that was a failure."

The father's face was creased with questions. "Special service group? Never heard of such a thing. When did you get out?"

"Only a few months ago."

"What rank were you? I made sergeant before my enlistment ran out."

"I was a major."

"I'll ask my friend Charlie about you. He knows most of the military men around here. Do you know Charlie Davies?"

"Never heard of him. Listen, it's getting late. I have to be heading home." He stood up and gave Mary a slight bow.

She stood up. "I'll see you out."

In the doorway, she whispered, "Sorry about my father. He's a little obsessed with military things."

"It was not a problem. May I call on you again sometime?"

"Yes, that would be delightful."

Chapter Thirty-Six

On the way home, Dalton thought about the visit. He had done everything right, per the book, but the father had come in and ruined it all. Per the book, that wasn't supposed to happen. Parents listening in was expected, but coming in and taking over the conversation wasn't. He shook his head. *Her father is a Civil War veteran. How's that possible?*

The last part of his trek was by trolley. He jumped off at the stop nearest his home. It was getting dark, by the time he climbed the steps to his apartment. He was hungry and didn't have much to eat, so he snacked on some fruit before going to bed.

He sat tossing and turning, upset by reminders of just how far back in time he had traveled. He had known better than to take this mission, when he found out he was the one who built the general's house in the Hamptons. *R. Adalwolf Dalton. Who else could that be?* Stupid. Would he have ruined time if he hadn't gone back? Did he ruin time by going back? He had ruined time once. Was he doing it again? Sometime after midnight, he fell into a fitful sleep.

After the weekend, Dalton came to the office. He was happy after a sunny Sunday. Summer had just started. When he passed by Mary's desk, however, he did a double take. Her eyes were bloodshot.

"What's the matter?"

She took in a deep breath. "Father says I can't see you anymore because you're a fraud."

"What?" He couldn't believe what he was hearing.

"He talked to his buddy at church on Sunday. He says Charlie would know all the majors in the army, but he didn't know you. Daddy says people like you never served in the army, but want the glory associated with being a veteran."

Robert folded his arms. He hadn't realized he wouldn't be taken at face value. This was a crisis and he didn't know how to get out of it. "Who is this Charlie, anyway, who's supposed to know everything?"

"He works in the adjutant general's office."

"I see." He looked her in the eyes, and said, "I promise you that I was in the military. There will be no record of me at the army or navy, because I didn't serve with either of those. I was in a special branch working on a top secret project. I can't tell you anymore than that."

"I told Daddy he was wrong. I saw the sadness in your eyes when you talked about how your friend was killed. I told him, but he wouldn't listen."

"Thank you for believing me. I would like to see you again. What can we do?"

"You can talk to Daddy. He isn't always right, you know."

"I can't prove to him I served in the military. What can I do?"

"Please try."

Jim nodded. It was going to be tough to talk to the old man, but he had to try, because he didn't want to lose her. "I'll come calling next Friday. I'll talk to him then."

She stood up and kissed him on the cheek. "Thank you."

Dalton sighed. Facing her father was going to be awkward, at best. He didn't think it would help. Still, he liked the girl and there must be something to it. According to Ross, he would get married and have kids while he was here. At least the real R. Adalwolf Dalton would, if that was indeed him and not some strange coincidence.

The work was busy all that week. Mary smiled at him every time he arrived at the office.

When Friday came, Ted gave him a large amount of money. "You've earned it. You are the best trader I've ever seen. Even better than I am. Keep up the good work."

"I thought you were angry for the personal trades." Ted had barely talked to him all week.

"I'm still waiting to see if those pan out, but it looks good so far."

Dalton smiled. He left Ted to lock up. He had to get to the clothing store before they closed. He wanted to impress Mary, at least. It might be his last chance.

When he arrived at Mary's home, it was her father who came to the door. Robert could see Mary behind him. She looked sad.

"Well, if it isn't the imposter. I had Charlie check the military records, and you don't exist. You were never in the Army."

"No, Sir, I was never in the army."

"So you admit it."

"I do, but I never said I was in the army. I wasn't in the navy, either. I said I was in the armed forces, and I was a major."

Her father was silent. He stared at Dalton trying to figure out what he just said. He was quiet for a second. "I thought there was only the army and the navy. Isn't that all the armed services?"

"No, Sir, there is the Air Force. I was a major in the Air Force."

This seemed to really perplex Mary's father. "But, I've never heard of it."

"That's because I was part of a top secret mission. I'm the only representative of the Air Force that's left. The others were left behind or killed. I cannot tell you any more about it."

Her father stood there for a few minutes, then smiled. "All I have to say is that if you're telling the truth, then I'm impressed with you. If that's a lie, and I can't prove it either way, then that's the most imaginative lie I've heard in a long, long time. Come in, Mary's waiting for you."

Chapter Thirty-Seven

Summer ebbed into fall and Dalton called upon Mary more and more. She was twenty-one and not married. Dalton blamed her overbearing father for that. Her brother referred to her as Old Maid Mary. Nothing else mattered to Dalton. He had found love, something that made his banishment to the past more tolerable. He proposed in September, her family prepared for a spring wedding. The two of them were sitting on the front porch one day, watching the fall colors when she asked. "I haven't met your family yet. When are you going to introduce me?"

He sighed heavily. "I don't have a family."

Her brow furloughed in a question. "You don't have a family? No mother or father? Are they dead?"

He turned to look her in the eyes. "I can't lie to you, but you wouldn't understand. I don't belong in the here and now. I'm a soul adrift."

She slowly shook her head. "A sad soul you are. What happened to your family? Can you tell me?"

"The truth is, I don't know. I will never know. There was a time I had a mother and a father and I grew up in a nice home. Times have changed and I was ripped from my happy life. I no longer know anything about them. How they are doing and where they are, they've been told I'm dead, I suppose."

"That is so sad. Have you looked for them?"

"I can't explain it, but it's of no use. I wouldn't find them."

She hugged him. "I'm so sorry. You live a life of sadness. Your friend died and your family is lost to you. How do you bear it?"

"You. I have you now. That is how I bear it. I've never loved another woman but you."

She leaned over and squeezed him tight.

Her father came out on the porch and cleared his throat, so she sat up.

"Well, I must be going." He stood up and put on his hat. He hated the thing, but everyone around him was wearing one and he didn't want to look out of place, even though he was.

"Goodbye, Sweetheart," Mary said.

"You have a good day Adalwolf," her father replied.

He started going by the name Adalwolf. It would be a signal to his future self that he was there. His soon to be father-in-law respected that and referred to him by that name. Mary didn't. To her, he would always be Robert.

He took the normal route back to town. He was spending so much time at Mary's that her family was asking him to meals. Her mother was a wonderful cook, but her younger brother was a terrible tease. It was he who had alerted the father that they were hugging too close, he was sure of it. The brother watched them like a hawk.

Dalton was buying more and more stock. He was getting quite the portfolio, which wasn't going unnoticed by Ted. He didn't seem to mind, as he had at first. He would advise his clients to purchase the same stocks as Dalton.

The next morning, when Dalton walked into the office, Ted was standing by Mary's desk. He had his arms folded.

"Good morning Ted, Mary," Dalton said. He knew something was up, but let it play out instead of forcing it.

"It's war. The Boers ignored the ultimatum. There is fighting in Africa." Ted picked up the paper from the table and showed it to Dalton.

"War is never good."

"But you knew it would happen."

"It has been brewing for a long time."

Ted wanted to tell Dalton he had a smudged piece of paper that spelled out the exact day the war would start, but held his tongue. There were a lot of other intriguing events to go through before he would pin Adalwolf down on how he knew about it all. There were a lot more improbable events on it than a war that had been predicted for a long time. Still, knowing the exact day that the war would start was intriguing.

"What should we do now, buy more steel stock?"

"No, sell and buy Springfield rifle stock. They are on the verge of something big."

"Springfield, it is."

Chapter Thirty-Eight

It was the happiest day in his life, seeing his bride in her silk dress, with flowers in her hair and spring in the air. The day had arrived. They held it in a church in the center of town. The large church would be there a hundred and thirty years later. He used to walk by it on the way to the office. He had no idea what it would mean to him in his future past. His new-old life, he would call it. Old because it was yesteryear, new because he had found love.

The organ played The Wedding March as Mary came down the aisle with her father. He was in an army uniform. It wasn't his original one, but it was exactly the same, only larger to fit his widening girth. He had tried to talk Dalton into wearing one also, but Dalton told him his was at the bottom of the Atlantic Ocean. He wore a tuxedo.

Mary was in a long flowing dress, its silk train trailing ten feet behind her, with a lacy white veil.

The music stopped as she stood next to him. The priest was speaking, but Dalton was mesmerized by her eyes, and her happy smile. She had to pinch him when the priest asked him if he took her to wife.

"Ow, Oh, I do."

The rest was a blur except for the part where she said, "I do," and kissed him.

Many of the family friends had been seated on his side of the aisle, so everyone wouldn't be on the same side. He looked down and saw Charlie in the audience. Robert knew he was being scowled at. Charlie had told George, Dalton's soon to be father-in-law Dalton was a fraud many times. It was causing a rift in the family. Today he wouldn't worry about it.

Dalton danced with his new bride at the reception. A new life, a new bride and a new century. It wasn't his century, but it would hold no major surprises. After the reception, The Daltons took the train up to what would some day be known as the Hamptons. They arrived at the hotel after dark. It was a two story wood building with an old fading sign that said 'Orient Bay House.'

The couple was not paying any attention to anyone that night, but wrapped blissfully in each other's arms.

They overslept, and as Mary climbed out of bed and stretched, she looked around and said, "What is that horrible smell?"

Dalton sniffed the air. "Rotting fish?"

"It reeks."

Getting dressed, they headed down stairs to the desk. "What smells so bad?" Dalton asked the clerk.

"Sorry, Sir, it's the smell of spring, I'm afraid. The farmers use fish from the local sea food plants to fertilize their fields."

"Where can we go to get away from it?"

"It's not so bad by the beach. The only way to truly get away from it is to go back into the city."

"We may have to do that."

Mary smiled, "Let's at least give the beach a try before we give up. Come on, let's get our swim clothes on."

Dalton complied and soon the two of them were splashing in the waves along the coast.

After swimming for a couple of hours, they headed back to the hotel to change and then get something to eat.

The same clerk was at the desk when they passed by. "See, Sir, it doesn't smell so bad now, as long as the wind comes in from the sea and not out across the farm land."

"When does the wind usually change direction?"

"Evening."

He turned to Mary. "I want to show you something, then we can go back to the city to avoid the smell."

"Is it a surprise?"

"Yes. A very big one at that."

The two walked about a mile up from the hotel. When they arrived at a large spacious field, he stopped. "Well, what do you think?"

"What do I think about what?"

"This is ours. This plot of land, we own it. I'm going to build a large house on it, just like the one you live in now."

Her jaw dropped. "You bought a house in the middle of the stink?"

He laughed. "It won't stink in the future, and we don't live here yet, but we will someday."

She went deathly silent, as she stared at him. He turned towards her and could sense something wrong. "I'm sorry, I should have asked. I didn't mean to upset you."

"Robert, it isn't the land that I'm upset about. You keep talking about the future. You know things that are going to happen. You predicted when the Boer War would start, to the day. Ted showed me the paper."

"What paper?"

"The first day you worked for Ted, you made a mess of a piece of paper and threw it away. You asked for a new pen, but I knew you had never written with a fountain pen before. You held it differently. You know nothing about etiquette, which I found very odd for an officer and a gentleman. Over and over again, you say, 'It will be fine in the future,' and you knew what stocks to buy to make you the most money."

"I've never lied to you or your father."

"Tell me, my husband. What is the Air Force? What was your mission? How did it fail? How did you come to have no family, and why do you know the future? I'm your wife now. I need to know." She folded her arms.

He looked at her with pleading eyes. "Please don't think me insane when I tell you this." She didn't respond so he took a deep breath. "I am Robert Adalwolf Dalton, as you know. What you don't know is that I was born in Woodstock, Vermont on September 4th..." He paused for a second. "In the year 2001."

Her eyes went round as saucers. "What?"

He held up his hand. "Let me finish. I was sent back in time in a ship that flies through the air. In just a few years the Wright brothers will experiment with manned flight. By the time World War One comes around, they will use those airplanes as weapons. I was sent back in time to stop a monster from starting World War Two and killing millions of people. Our mission was a failure. We destroyed time rather than helped it. My airplane was damaged and I couldn't use it to get across the Atlantic, so I ditched it in the sea, along with my friend Captain Myers."

She took a few steps back, like she was ready to flee.

He continued, "That's why I have no family. They aren't born yet. My grandparents aren't born yet, and maybe even my great grandparents aren't born yet. Everyone I have even known is either dead, or not born yet. I'm all alone."

He sat down dejectedly on the ground. He had wrapped words around his sadness. It hit him like a ton of bricks. If she left, he would have no one. He wouldn't run after her, he would just let her go.

He just knew her father would say, 'See, I told you he was a fraud.'

He buried his head in his hands and sighed heavily.

He felt her hand on his shoulder, then she sat down on the ground next to him and put her arm around his waist. "Like my father says, if that's a lie, it's the best lie I've ever heard."

He looked up and kissed her. "It isn't a lie."

She thought for a minute. "Tell me more about these World Wars you mention, oh, and I want to hear about your mission, too."

"But if we don't move before the wind changes, it will stink again."

"I don't care about the stink. We have to get used to it, anyway, if we're going to live out here. We have all night, so start talking."

Chapter Thirty-Nine

Mary woke up to the same stench as the morning before. Yawning and stretching, she climbed out of bed. Dalton was still asleep and she smiled down at his prone figure. It did her good to know that the man was soft hearted enough not to let a four-year-old die. Well, the second time at least. Looking out the window, she tried to envision how the area would look years from now. The way he had described it, with upscale houses and small resort towns, it sounded beautiful. *And no stink, that's the best part.*

Did she believe him? She had gone over and over in her mind every word he had ever said to her. It was the only thing that could tie together everything he had ever told her. He had stuck to the same story the whole time, yet hadn't told her all of it until last night. He had risked losing her to answer the question. She had wanted to run, to bolt, so she could once again feel the sanity of the familiar, the here and now. Yet he had looked so pathetic. Why would he lie and chance that she would leave? He had crumpled to the ground when he had finished his tall tale. At that moment she had wanted to believe him. She would. She had decided, right then and there, she would believe the story, no matter who ridiculed it, especially her father.

He had talked about world wars and cold wars, and men on the moon. It had all been so fantastical. It was like a fiction novel. It would be scary if it all came true, and she believed it would.

Not being able to stand the stench any longer, she shook Dalton awake.

He looked up with blood shot eyes. "Huh?"

"Let's go back to the city and get some breakfast. Some place that doesn't remind me of rotting fish."

He gave the air a sniff. "I agree."

His stomach growled on the way back into the city on the train. They stopped north of town and found a diner to eat at. Afterwards, they made their way to the new apartment Dalton had rented. It was farther from work, but a street car ride wouldn't hurt him. It was a more spacious with new furniture. The stove was larger and it had windows facing east and west so they could have a cross breeze through the rooms during the summer. Still, Dalton was not spending a lot of money on it, compared to his income. He would have a nice nest egg by the time they moved out to the Hamptons.

They had been in their new place about a week, when the in-laws came to visit the newlyweds. George had no smile on his face. They had come when they knew Dalton wouldn't be home from work yet.

"Hello, Daddy, Mother." Mary hugged both of them.

George stood tall and straight, the way he always did when he was about to say something important. "Mary, Charles talked to the Secretary of War and he assured him, there is no organization called the Air Force. I'm afraid your Adalwolf has lied to us all."

She smiled, which surprised her father. "Of course, he didn't lie. Robert always tells the truth." She sat down in the front room and asked them to sit.

Her father was red faced. "But, but, Charles talked to the Secretary of War himself."

"I'm sure he did, only he talked to the wrong Secretary of War."

Her mother was in between them. She sat down and said, "Honey, do we have to talk about this now?"

"The wrong Secretary of War? We only have one Secretary of War."

Dalton walked in. "Oh, you're here already."

Her father was still red faced. "I believe you lied to us, Adalwolf."

"No, Sir, certainly not."

"Charles talked to the Secretary of War, the only Secretary of War, and he said there is no such thing as the Air Force."

Dalton sighed, cleared his throat, and shrugged. Mary smiled at him. "You are correct. Currently, there is no United States Air Force. It won't be organized until 1947."

Still red faced, her father was staring at him. "But, but, how do you know that?"

"That's just history, I mean, it will be history. It's history to me anyway. To you, it hasn't happened yet."

Her father was clutching his heart. He looked over at his wife, she was pale, as if she was about to faint.

"Perhaps a drink is in order. I don't think you're going to like the explanation of what Robert just said." Mary stood up and brought out a bottle of bourbon and four glasses.

Her father sat down in a chair next to his wife.

After Mary poured them each a glass, she sat down. "Well, Honey. You were saying?"

"I am Major Robert Adalwolf Dalton. Service date June 15, 2022. I was born in 2001. I was flying an airplane, which hasn't been invented yet, that could go back in time. A time machine. It was damaged and crashed in the middle of the Atlantic Ocean. I lost my co-pilot, Captain Myers."

George drained his glass and then held it out to be refilled. Mary obliged. He drained it again.

Her mother sat there in total shock.

It was quiet in the house for a few minutes, then the father turned to Mary. "You believe all this?"

"Certainly, I do."

Finally catching her breath, the mother asked, "Do you think they will come back in time to rescue you?" She was still very pale.

"No, there is only one time machine and it's on the bottom of the Atlantic."

Her father had regained his breath. "Can you prove any of this?"

"Yes, President McKinley will win the election this year."

"Almost anyone but his opponent William Bryan, could predict that."

"Yes, but he will be shot in the fall of next year and Theodore Roosevelt will become president."

Her father sat there a minute before saying, "Fair enough, we'll put you to the test."

Chapter Forty

A few weeks later when Dalton arrived at work, Ted was standing by Mary's old desk, waiting for him. He hadn't replaced her after she quit to get married.

"Hello, Robert."

"Hello. Are we trading today?"

"No. I've sold the business to a larger firm. Here's your last payday." He handed him a stack of money.

Dalton looked down at it. "This is short notice. What am I supposed to do for a job?"

Ted laughed. "We both know you don't need one. In fact, I started trading my own money using your tips. I won't need to work again, either. That's why I sold out."

Dalton nodded.

Ted handed him a wrinkled piece of paper, Dalton looked down on it. "I also used this to guide me. When you have someone who knows the future, it's easy to make money."

Dalton didn't know what to say. It was that first list he made of upcoming events in time, the one he had smudged and thrown away. He worried, he had ruined time.

"How do you do it, Robert? How do you know the future?"

Dalton smiled. "I can't tell you."

"You mean you won't tell me. It doesn't matter," Ted took the list back. "I still have this. It's been right every time. I can use it to guide me. I just have a few questions. What is a World War and what does Black Monday mean?"

"A World War means that almost every nation in the world is involved. The fact that it happens twice is a reflection on man's stupidity. Black Monday is the day the stock market crashes. A lot of people will lose their fortunes that day."

"I see, there are rough times ahead. Well, we'll worry about those later. Today, it's just you and me, and handful of cash and a chance to paint the town red. I'm buying."

That brought a smile to Dalton's face. "I'm in."

Three hours later, Dalton came home to his apartment. He surprised Mary, who didn't expect to see him for hours. "Ted sold the company. I'm out of a job."

Her eyes widened. "Do you need me to go back to work?"

"No, the truth is, I have a lot of friends on the floor of the exchange. I could find work tomorrow if I had to. No, I think we'll be okay if my investments pan out."

She put her hands on her hips. "If you know what's going to happen, why would you even say something like that?"

He smiled, she was so darling, even upset. "My investments will pan out. We still have to build that house in the Hamptons."

"Can we wait until they stop fertilizing with the fish?"

"Of course. In twenty years, it'll be the place to be."

Dalton took the next few months to work on his stock portfolio. He would sell some of the shares when they reached their high point. Ted selling the company had put a damper on his ready cash, but didn't hurt him otherwise. It was time, he knew, to invest in munitions. He did it a little at a time, so as not to be noticed by others. Living frugally helped, and Mary never complained. When the fall came, McKinley won handily.

"No surprise there," George said. A few days after President McKinley was shot, the couple was visited by Dalton's in laws.

"You were wrong, Adalwolf. He was shot, but not killed." George hadn't even made it all the way through the door when he said it. Mary stepped out of the way and let him enter.

"He will come down with an infection tomorrow, and die the next day. All from the gunshot wound," Dalton said as he looked up.

Having the wind briefly taken out of his sails, Mary's father replied, "But they say he's getting better."

"Wait until tomorrow."

"Until tomorrow then," he replied. Despite the ongoing conflict between the two men, they were civil when they sat down for dinner. Mary had managed to come up with a meal despite having her parents drop by unexpectedly.

The next day, they didn't hear from George. When the paper arrived a day later she read it to Dalton. "President McKinley is dead."

"It brings me no joy to say I was right. I don't think your father will bother me again about being a major in the Air Force."

She didn't respond, just kept looking down at the paper. "Could you have stopped it?"

He realized how upset she was. "Could I have, yes. Will I going forward, no. I changed history once already. It was a terrible thing to do. I saved millions of lives, only to have billions of people die. I'm not a god. I can't make decisions about who lives and who dies. I will stay on the sidelines and hope for the best."

She dropped the paper and rushed into his arms to cry. "Knowing is worse than not knowing. I sat by and let someone get murdered. Not only someone, but the President of the United States. That's not the worst of it. We will sit by and let others get murdered, starting wars that will kill millions. How can we stand ourselves?"

Dalton held her, not knowing what to say.

Chapter Forty-One

"Do you smell that?" Dalton asked.

"I just smell the salt air." Mary teased. She knew what he was getting at, but wasn't playing along.

"No rotting fish. All of the fish processors have moved away."

She sniffed the air. "Yes, I love it. When do we move here?"

"I'm working with the builder. He should start soon."

She looked around, "This is really a beautiful place. Daddy would have loved that you modeled the home after the one he built."

He held her close. "Your father was a good man."

He flashed back to the funeral. George was buried in Arlington among many of his army friends, both those who died old and those who died young, twenty-one gun salute and all. When the folded flag was handed to Mary's mother, she cried. That was months ago. Her mother had sold the house to the ever expanding city. It was torn down and apartments already replaced it. Moving back into an almost identical house would be a blessing to mother and daughter.

"This will be so nice. Calm, compared to the city life. Mother will love it here."

Dalton cleared his throat. "Will your mother be all right if we take a little trip?"

Mary turned to face him. "Yes, I'll have my brother look after her. Where are we going?"

"I have to go back to Germany. A cruise down the Danube would be wonderful."

She jumped up and clapped her hands. "The Danube! That's sounds wonderfully romantic."

"I've also some unfinished business there. I have to visit Passau. I left some books buried in the woods. I want to retrieve them before the world devolves into chaos and war."

Her forehead creased. "Are you sure they'll be there after all these years?"

He held her hand and walked towards the train station. "It's only been six years. The books are the ones I stole out of the library in Germany. They tell of the history I've prevented. One of these days, I'll write the story of the mission and leave it in the place where the general can find it."

She looked up at him as they were walking. "How are you going to do that?"

"It's an interesting story. The house we build will be sold after we're gone. It's hit by a hurricane and damaged. After it's abandoned, a group of teenagers use it for parties. They accidentally set it on fire, so it's damaged more."

"Our home is going to be destroyed in the future?" Her voice was full of emotion.

"The story gets better. The general buys the house and restores it. If I can put the report somewhere in the house where he'll find it, then I'll be able to tell him to scratch the project."

"How do you know he will buy the house in the future? What if time changes and he doesn't?"

"I can only hope he does. He did last time. The historian on the project, Colonel Ross, said it happened that way. The only thing is, he didn't find any report on his property. I'm going to do it anyway. It's worth a try."

She squeezed his hand. "I hope, someday, you will forget the future and start living in the present."

"I don't know. Knowing the future has made us a lot of money."

She smiled, "It has."

When they arrived at the station, they only had to wait a few minutes before the train came.

As they sat down she asked, "When are we going to Germany?"

"As soon as I can arrange it. I don't know what ships are going across and how long they are going to take to do it."

"So, how would you get there, if we were in your time?"

"We would take a plane, be there in seven or eight hours."

Her mouth gaped open. "*Hours?*"

"Think of all the things you'll see. We might not live to see it, but they will put a man on the moon in the 1960s."

"Oh my, the moon, how do they do that?"

"They will build a really big rocket."

They hadn't noticed the man who had sat down behind them. He had a hat pulled down to his eyebrows. He had been watching them for some time. Pulling out a pad, the man wrote a note.

Ted

I found them. They are buying property and building a house on Long Island, east of the city. I suggest you do too. He's talking about the future, but I'm having a hard time hearing him over the train noises. Something about airplanes and sending a man to the moon.

Bill

Chapter Forty-Two

Dalton looked up at the mast full of sails. RMS *Etruria* was a steam powered ship with two enormous funnels in the middle of her, but she also relied on sail. The wind was favorable so the captain had elected to cut the steam and man the sails. Men had run every which direction in an organized chaos. They knew what to do though. Soon sails appeared and filled with the evening wind. It was like organized chaos.

He thought about the men working the boilers and how they were now able to take a break. His few days down there forever changed him. He now knew hard work and camaraderie. No one could understand what it was like, if they had never been through it.

Mary slipped her hand in his. "There you are. I've been looking all over for you."

He smiled down at her. "I've never sailed the seas before. I've flown over them, but never upon them. I'm loving this." He was happy inside. He wanted a second class cabin, but his wife talked him into a first class one. They were treated like kings.

"Why do they need ships when those planes you told me about can fly between cities in a matter of hours?"

"They aren't so much for transportation, but enjoyment. They have live shows, and large restaurants. There are all sorts of things to do on them."

"How big are they?"

"Huge, some hold up to six thousand passengers."

Her eyes went wide open. "Six thousand. Do they stack them in like cord wood?"

Dalton let out a brief laugh. "No, nothing like that. Everyone has their own cabins, with a private toilet in it, soft beds and furniture. I hear they're quite nice."

"It's still way too many people. It sounds like a floating city."

"It is."

"Not for me."

He watched the ocean rush past the bow and again looked up at the masts. It was good to feel the wind in his hair. "Beautiful, isn't it?"

"Such a lovely ship."

They walked around to the other side of the ship. Nothing was visible, just the vast ocean.

"Do you miss the future? Do you wish you could go back?"

"Some things, yes. I miss being able to look things up without going to the library. I miss some of the foods. I miss cars, but most of all, I miss flying."

"It must be hard for you."

"No, I miss those things, but I can live without them. I never knew how lonely I was until I met you. You are the light of my life."

She smiled up at him. "It's about to be less lonely for you."

"What do you mean?"

"I'm pregnant."

His mouth gaped open. "What? I mean, that's wonderful."

"You must have known all this already, even whether it's a boy or girl. Maybe even the name."

"No, I wasn't told any of that. When's it due?"

"Not until May of next year. I don't know anything about raising children. What if I don't do a good job?"

"You have your mother to help you. She did a great job of raising you."

She smiled, "You are so sweet."

He hugged her. On the way back to the cabin, he passed a man. He could swear he'd seen the face before, but couldn't place it. Dalton was about to turn around and speak to the man, but he had already ducked around the corner. He scratched his head.

"Everything all right, Honey?" Mary asked.

"Yes, of course. I'm going to be a father." He smiled down at her. He did glance back in the hopes of seeing the man one more time, but he didn't reappear. *It's a small ship. He can't hide forever.*

They headed down the steps into the corridor and then to their stateroom. It had red carpeting, an overstuffed chair and a large, Victorian style couch. The bed was one of the softest he had ever slept on. Dalton pulled out a piece of paper from the desk drawer. He wrote down the man's physical description, then sat back and tried to remember where he had seen him before. It suddenly came to him. "The train on Long Island. He was the man on the train."

Chapter Forty-Three

A nightmare raged in Dalton's mind. "Are you ready to go back?" The man in the suit kept asking him over and over again.

"I have to take her with me."

"You can't, she will not adapt to the 21st century."

"She's my wife."

"Are you ready to go back?"

"I'm not leaving."

"My orders are to take you back with me, Major Dalton. We can do it the easy way, and you come willingly, or the hard way, and I taser you and stuff you in the back of the plane. Which shall it be?"

Dalton sat straight up in bed. He was in a cold sweat and his heart was racing. Going over to the basin, he washed his face. *I'm not leaving without her.*

Getting dressed, he decided to go up on deck to get some fresh air. Outside, looking at the waves was the man who had been following Mary and him. He walked up next to the man. "Nice night."

The man jumped a little when he saw Dalton. "Ah, yes. Nice night. You startled me."

Dalton cleared his throat. "Why are you following me?"

"I don't know what you mean, Sir." The man started walking away, but Dalton caught him by the arm, and using a joint manipulation technique he learned in the Air Force, he pinned the man to the wall.

"Why are you following me? Are you here to bring me back?"

"You're breaking my arm."

"Start talking and I'll stop breaking."

"All right, I'll tell you, just let me go."

Dalton released his grip, but stood close to the man so he could catch him, if he tried to run.

"It's Ted, your former boss. He's hired me to follow you. He's nuts, but he pays well. Says you got some sort of machine that you can see the future with. He wants it."

Dalton's shoulders relaxed. "You're going all the way across the Atlantic Ocean for that?"

"Aye, Sir."

"Tell Ted, my crystal ball has broken in a million pieces and sunk into the middle of the ocean."

"Aye, Sir, I will, Sir." The man turned and walked away.

Dalton calmed down by watching the ocean glide by. The sails had been tied up and the steam engines were billowing out smoke. After taking a few minutes, he headed back to his cabin. He slipped in quietly. Luckily Mary was still asleep, so he slipped back into bed. He was finally able to get some sleep.

The next morning, the sunshine shone bright and the sails were spread again. Dalton looked out the porthole and wished he were up on deck.

"Good morning," Mary said as she stretched and yawned. Sitting up in bed she asked, "Did you sleep well?"

"On the second try. How did you sleep?"

"Like a rock. I'm starving, though. Let's go eat."

"I'm all for that. Let's go."

She jumped out of bed and dressed quickly. As they walked down to breakfast she rubbed her stomach. "I'm eating for two, you know."

"I totally understand."

"Totally? You say the strangest things."

He realized it was a new expression she might not have heard before. "It's hard for me to take my language skills back a hundred years, but I'll try."

"It seems to me, if you use words like that, then the language is going backwards, not forwards."

He smiled. "I'll grant you that."

"Grant you that?"

"Never mind. What shall we have for breakfast?"

She laughed. "The future has strange language indeed."

They walked hand in hand. He gave up on talking for the time being. When they were seated, he looked over and saw Ted's spy watching him. Dalton tipped his hat to him and the man responded in kind.

"Who was that?"

"Oh, just a man I talked to up on deck."

"You have a good conversation?"

"Yes, he was very interesting."

The waiter came up and took their order. Dalton sat back in the chair and stretched out. He was starting to get used to being where he was. *It isn't so bad after all. I do want a car though. Life would be so much easier if I had a car.* He started to think about when the model T would come out. *I need to invest in that.* He couldn't remember the exact year, but he knew it would be soon, very soon.

Chapter Forty-Four

It had been a long trip to Passau, but now Dalton, with his arm around Mary, watched the lights of the city grow larger as they approached it from around the bend in the river. It was the last leg of their outbound journey. Dalton decided to spend a few nights in the city before going home.

It seemed like a century ago since he had last been there, yet it had only been a few years. He shuddered inside as they approached. The young boy, Hitler, must still live there. What would he do if he ran into him again? He shook the thoughts from his mind.

The travel must have been taking a toll on his pregnant wife. She said she loved it, but morning sickness had set in and she was swelling up in the summer heat. She was a trooper though, never complaining.

As the ship approached the dock, workers caught the lines and fastened them to the pier. The couple gathered up their things and headed down.

Mary smiled as she stepped ashore. "It's beautiful here."

"You've said that about every town we've been through."

"There are a lot of beautiful places, and this is one of them."

Dalton carried their bags up the street. He knew of only one hotel so he decided to stay there again. The desk clerk greeted them and had a bell hop take the bags up to their room. After the boy left, they sat down in their room, relaxing after the long trip.

"It so nice you speak German. It's so much easier. We had such a hard time communicating in France. None of them seemed to know a word of English."

"That was why I was recruited for the mission. I speak fluent German."

She turned, sadness shown in her eyes. "This is where it all happened, isn't it? It must be hard for you to come back here. Your friend was killed here."

"No, he was dead by the time we arrived back here. He was shot miles from here. I'm not sure where he died, somewhere in southern Germany."

"Is it hard being back?"

He nodded. He didn't trust his voice to tell her how hard it was. After swallowing, he said. "Let's go to bed. I want to get some sleep, and then tomorrow after breakfast, I need to go recover those books."

"I hope they're still there, for your sake."

"For the future's sake. It will talk them out of trying again."

She gasped, putting her hand up to her mouth. "You don't think they'll come for you? I mean, build another time machine and return to this time?"

The nightmare flashed in his mind of him being taken back without her. "No," he said simply, but not convincingly. "I'll have to write that report and leave it where they will find it, otherwise they might take us to a place we don't want to be."

She was shaking, so he sat beside her and held her. "It will take a lot of money and time to build another time machine, and they don't have either. We'll be alright."

She nodded her head, but was still shaking. "What if they find the old one and repair it?"

That was something he had thought about. He didn't know how deep the ocean was where he ditched the plane. If it was on the continental shelf, then it wasn't too deep. If not, it would be very hard to recover until the 21st century. By then, the corrosion would have caused the plane to be a total loss.

"I can tell by your silence that it is a possibility."

He met her gaze. "I was just thinking about that. I'll leave where the plane is out of my report. The ocean's a very big place, even for modern man."

"Yes, leave that part out. Let's raise our children and grow old together in this century. It's brand new, and so far, there's nothing wrong with it. If you get a chance, however, I want you to find and destroy that thing."

"Yes, I promise."

She turned and hugged him. He held her until her shoulders relaxed.

Chapter Forty-Five

After buying a shovel in town, the couple headed across the foot bridge and up the hill to find the spot where the books were buried. It was a warm, cloudless day, as they headed into the forest.

Dalton walked around for a long time. "Everything has changed. I can't find the spot."

"Did you mark it at all?"

"I have the GPS coordinates for it, but the GPS sank with the plane."

Her eyes narrowed. "You're doing it again. What's a GPS?"

He looked up and gave her a sheepish smile. "Global Positioning Satellite. It's how we know where we are in the future."

"Can't you just look around and say, 'Oh, here I am?'"

"It's a little more complex than that." He looked down at his feet and noticed the ground was lower than the surrounding earth. "Oh, here I am."

She let out a stifled laugh. Ignoring her, he began to dig. Soon the shovel hit something solid, so he knelt down and moved the dirt away with his hands. Soon, he pulled up a rubberized waterproof sack. He brushed the rest of the soil off of it.

"What's that?" she asked.

"It's a zipper." He zipped the bag open and pulled out the books and the money.

She moved closer to get a better look at the bag. When he zipped it close, her eyes widened in delight. "Oh, my. Can I play with it?"

He handed her the bag. "It'll replace buttons in the near future."

She began zipping it open and then closed. "That is amazing. When can I start using this on my clothes?"

"Pretty soon, I think. I don't know everything about every invention."

He turned to leave, but she was still playing with the zipper. "Hide that thing. We don't want to draw any attention to ourselves."

"Sorry." She handed it back to him and he put it under his arm. Leaving the shovel there, they headed back into town.

Back at the hotel, Dalton stuffed the bag in his suitcase. Mary couldn't resist playing with the zipper one more time before he closed it.

"Do you mind?"

"But, it's fascinating."

With the bag stowed, the couple started down the stairs toward the street, on their way to dinner. Dalton spotted two men standing in the lobby of the hotel, staring at him.

They immediately looked away, which raised his suspicion. "Wait right here. Dear. I need to go get something out of the room."

He ran back up the stairs and grabbed the books out of the bag. He set them behind the chamber pot. Grabbing a few novels he had read on the way over, he put them in the bag and then zipped it back up. He put the money from the bag in his jacket pocket.

Mary was waiting for him. The two men had sat down and were talking to each other. Dalton could hear their American accents. *Did Ted send others to spy on him also?* These two didn't look amateurish, like Ted's spy. They had been spotted only because they had just arrived at the hotel. *I'm just being paranoid.*

"Shall we go to dinner?"

"Sounds divine."

"I know of a place with wonderful wiener schnitzel."

"Never heard of it."

"It's very good."

After dinner they strolled back up to the hotel. When entering the room, Dalton noticed several things were out of place. He looked behind the chamber pot. The books were still there, but the suitcase was opened and the bag was missing.

Mary clutched her hand to her chest. "Someone's been in here. They took your books."

"No, my books are safe. I hid them. The two men in the lobby looked suspicious to me, so I came back up."

"What are they after?"

"I don't know. I think Ted might be behind this. There was a man on the ship who was following us. I caught him, but the first time I saw these two was today."

"Are we safe?"

"I don't know. We have return tickets on the ship going to Regensburg, but I think we'd better take the train instead. It will be faster and leaves a day earlier. If we can get ahead of them, they will never catch up."

Chapter Forty-Six

On the trip home, Dalton and Mary slept on trains as they raced through Europe. When they finally reached the coast, they boarded the first available steamer back to America. Even then, Dalton walked the ship, making sure that the two men who had followed them weren't on it. Finding no one suspicious, he settled in for an enjoyable ride home. Mary was extra tired and slept in most mornings. Dalton would bring her a tray around noon every day, so she wouldn't miss breakfast. He worried he had pushed her too hard.

When the ship docked in New York City, they made their way to the apartment. Mary's mother and brother were there.

There were greetings all around and Mary told them the good news about her pregnancy. They both hugged her.

That night, however, when Mary was in bed, her brother David took Dalton aside. "There have been men asking about you. Several of them have come to the apartment. It's upsetting Mother."

"I'm sorry. They are after something and they think I have it. My old boss might be the cause of all this misery. They followed us to Europe, even broke into the hotel room."

David's eyes widened. "What are you going to do?"

"I'll get two large dogs when the house in the Hamptons is complete. I'll make sure there is a distance between me and those who are bothering me."

Ted was eating his breakfast, at his usual café. A man came up and sat down across from him. Ted looked up. "Well, what did you find out?"

"He said his crystal ball was on the bottom of the Atlantic."

Ted took another bite. "I sent you all that way to find that out?"

"I found out more than that. Two other fellows were following this Adalwolf character. I overhead them on a couple of occasions. They were talking about a time machine."

Ted glanced up. "Who were they?"

"I don't know. Looked like some military types. The one called the other one 'sir' all the time."

"A time machine, eh? Makes more sense than a crystal ball. He's looking backwards in time, not forward."

"This is all crazy talk, you know."

Dalton pulled the paper from his pocket. It was the smudged one that Dalton had thrown away years earlier. "He's been able to predict all the important events in history, to the day. No, this isn't crazy."

The man looked at the paper. "So, what do we do now?"

"You need to lease us a ship. We are going looking for a time machine."

"But, boss. It's in the middle of the Atlantic Ocean."

"All we need to do is track the ship he came to America on, trace the route and figure out where he was picked up. That's where the time machine is."

"What?"

Ted sipped his coffee. "A ship picked him up from the middle of the ocean. His ship sank. I have the name of that ship on his employment application. All I need to do is figure out its route and where he was picked up."

"You're a genius."

Two men stood straight and tall in front of Charles Emerson, teeth clenched.

"You lost them? How could you do that?"

"Sir, he didn't board the ship like he was supposed to. He had tickets for it. By the time we realized it, he was several days ahead of us."

"Books, all you have is books? He dug up something from the woods. Where is that?"

The taller of the two men set the bag in front of him. Charles picked it up and looked at it. "I've never seen anything like this." One of the men showed him how to open it. He took the two novels out and put them on the desk.

"These must be written in code. I want you to go over every word and figure out what they really say, do you understand that? My friend George, before he died, confided in me that this man came from the future. He must have come here somehow."

The taller man swallowed hard. "Yes, Sir."

Charles cleared his throat. "And not a word of this to the Secretary of War. He already thinks I'm crazy."

"Yes, Sir."

Chapter Forty-Seven

"I can finish the north wing of the house at any time. There is no reason to wait." The builder was in his bib overalls. He was a tall muscular man with a bushy mustache and blonde hair. He wore a beret.

"I have to do one thing before that. Give me a couple of months and I'll be ready." Dalton looked up at the house. It was finished except for the one side where the general would build his den, a nearly perfect copy of the house that Mary had grown up in, except for the parlor. He hated parlors.

"I can at least finish the foundation by laying the slab for the chimney."

"No, I'll do that. I want to get my hands dirty. I'll contact you when I'm ready to finish."

The tall Swede scratched his head. "All right, it's just so close to being done."

"I know, and a beautiful house it is. You do good work. I'll be sure to tell anyone thinking of moving out here."

"Thank you, Sir."

The builder walked away, still scratching his head.

Mary stood in the doorway of their new home.

Dalton came up to her. "It's okay, go inside and look around. It's ours now."

"No, I want you to carry me across the threshold. It's more romantic that way."

Dalton smiled as he picked her up. "If my back breaks, I'm blaming you."

As they entered the house, her mother and brother were standing in the living room. "This is wonderful." The mother said.

"Where's my room?" David asked.

"Who says you're living here?" Dalton set Mary down. She reached up and kissed him.

"I'm your newest employee. Don't you want to treat me right?"

Dalton needed someone to look after his business interests in Europe. Since David was keen on traveling and Dalton was not, he had hired him. Now that he was out of school, he needed a job.

"Upstairs, first door to the left. The room with all your clothes in the closet."

"You had my things brought over?"

"Of course, as long as we were moving."

David ran up the stairs to look. Mary and her mother made their way to the kitchen.

"I see you've already been shopping. The pantry is full," her mother said.

"Robert and I went together."

"I just don't understand why you take that man with you. Your father would have sooner died than go to the market."

"Times are changing, Mother."

Her mother sighed but didn't respond, as the baby started crying. Mary ran into the living room to check on him. She picked up the child and then sat down to nurse him. David came running back down the stairs. "It's a good view, but why didn't you build closer to the beach?"

"Hurricanes." It wasn't a good excuse, since the house would be hit by one after he died, but he didn't want to tell David the truth. David knew a lot about what was going on, but not all.

"I hadn't thought about that."

David looked out the window to the front of the house where the Ford Model T was parked. "When are you going to teach me to drive?"

"In about fifty years."

"Oh, come on, Adalwolf."

"Someday, but not today. Is that better?"

"It's better than fifty years."

David ran off to explore the yard and Mary's mother was still in the kitchen, so Dalton sat down next to his wife and child.

"Are we happy here?" she asked. "What will become of us? Who will die first? Will I be able to raise my kids with two world wars looming?"

"Today is a happy day. Why are you so worried about the future?"

"I know too much about it."

"Your son will be too young for the first World War and too old for the second. David, on the other hand, might have to go, if drafted. I'm not sure how it works. I don't know who goes first, all I know is that I build this house and I've done that. I'm now going to finish up my report on the mission and bury it in the foundation with the hope that the general finds it someday."

She nodded, then looked back down at the baby. "Is there something you're not telling me?"

"Many things, but I don't think they involve us."

"I'm sorry for all these questions, it's just that, I'm worried."

"Don't worry, we'll live our lives and grow old together here. We won't move again."

Lifting the baby up to burp him, she said, "It's a lovely spot to grow old. I'm glad I met you, Robert Adalwolf Dalton."

Chapter Forty-Eight

Dalton sat at his desk finishing up his report. It had taken him several months to do it. Reading the books from Germany, he was convinced he did the right thing by not letting Adolf Hitler die. It would have been worse for the people of Europe otherwise. Twenty-three years of war had followed the elections in Germany when the communist party took over. The joining of forces between Russia and Germany had a chilling effect all over Europe. Soon the Balkans and then Scandinavia were under communist control. They didn't go peacefully. They fought, even after their governments surrendered. The partisan ruled the nights. Soon France and England came under attack. They too eventually succumbed to the communists.

That wasn't the end of it, however. Three times a fleet from Europe tried to invade the United States, twice from across the Atlantic and once from across the Bering Strait. The Atlantic fleets were defeated by a smaller, but more audacious, American Navy.

The United States had seen the buildup of ships and men in the eastern ports of Russia. When the communists struck, there was a naval force to oppose them. The Communists struggled to gain a foothold, capturing most of the Aleutian Islands. After a year, they gave up and retreated back to Russia.

Germany had become the dominate partner with its industrial might. Russia split up the alliance, causing a cross-border war. It killed millions and ended with a stalemate across the Russian winter ice. The Germans and the Russians were bitter foes after being allies for so long.

Heartened by their war against each other, all of the occupied states started rebelling, helped by American munitions smuggled into their countries.

A United States task force leap-frogged from northern Canada, through Greenland and Iceland, and landed in northern Norway. Scandinavia was soon free as the Germany troops fled back home. That was where the history book ended. He didn't know if the war was still going on, but seeing what a hot reception he had been given when he had flown into their airspace, he guessed it was. The book also told about mass executions by the Russians of captured German villages. Knowing the things that happened in the Second World War, he guessed the Germans weren't any more merciful.

Dalton shivered, thinking about the atrocities committed by both sides. Far more people had died than in the World War. He packed up the books into the metal box and David and he took it over to the foundation of the fireplace and set it in there. Then they poured the cement that David had mixed over it.

"Do you think anyone will ever find this?"

"I'm hoping so. It would have been a lot of work for nothing, otherwise."

"Time machine and adventures, It's an amazing tale."

Dalton grabbed a trowel and smoothed out the cement. He put a simple X in the middle of it. "Yes, an amazing tale."

David shook his head. "Here, let me try." He smoothed out the X and cut a better one in the cement. "You don't want them laughing at you when they find it."

Dalton admired it. "Good work."

The two men cleaned up then walked back into the house.

Mary had supper ready. "Is it done, then?"

"Yes, it's done. I'll get ahold of the builder tomorrow to finish the house. He was wanting to do it soon."
She nodded and set the dishes on the table.

Her mother came into the room, and they all sat down. It had been a long day.

After dinner, when the baby was put to bed, Mary and Dalton took a stroll down by the water, holding hands.

"Did you do the right thing? I mean, every day I look to the sky thinking, I might see that airplane come down that's going to take you away from me."

"I won't go. If they find this, it should be enough to stop them from trying again. The plane was very expensive. They won't be able to come up with the money anytime soon."

"They could come get you before we met. You would gladly go then, while you're in the water, awaiting rescue. Now that they know how to time travel, they could do whatever they want. What would my life be without you?"

"I guess you'd be working for Ted still. He wouldn't have near the money that he has now." He stopped on the beach and kissed her. "I'm glad I met you, Mary Dalton. These have been the happiest days of my lives."

"Lives?"

"I meant life. Freudian slip."

"A what?"

"Never mind. I guess Doctor Freud isn't famous yet. If you think about it, lives is correct, because the two centuries I've lived in are completely different."

"Yes, but please, stay in my world."

Chapter Forty-Nine

Ross set the report down. "Well, gentlemen, that's the end of the story. The mission didn't fail. It succeeded at first, but the officer in charge made a judgment call."

"Where does that leave us?" the general asked.

"It is our duty to find that airplane and destroy it. The potential to do massive damage, while attempting to do good, could be catastrophic, like it was the first time. We are talking end of the world possibilities. Look what the difference of even one four-year-old boy makes."

"What will we do for a budget? Senator James has cut our funding."

Ross thought for a moment. "I can stall him a couple of months. Meanwhile, we can get your hard drive out of storage, and using the information that Dalton gave us, we take into account wind, weather and tides to figure out where the most likely final resting place of the plane is."

"Yes, Sir."

Ross turned to the general. "You can work on the outside by getting us a boat with side-scanning sonar. Those costs must not be reported. So I can hide some money in another budget category to cover that."

"I'm on it. It's good to be working again."

"I think we should meet at the general's house from now on. It might raise suspicion to see him around here talking to us.

"That's fine by me," Williams replied.

Dempsey nodded in agreement.

"Fine, let's meet in about a month from now. That should give us enough time to do what we need to do."

"Yes, Sir," Dempsey replied.

Senator James walked into Lieutenant General Max Parker's office like he owned the place. "Project Black Hole hasn't been shut down yet." He said, while standing there waiting for an answer, his arms folded. It was more of an accusation than a statement.

"Well, Senator, there is a lot of paperwork to do with a shutting down of a project. All the equipment has to be accounted for and reports written." The general disliked the senator. The fact that James controlled the purse strings to most of the Air Force projects wasn't lost on him, however.

"They brought back that modeler." Another accusation.

Colonel Ross had told the general why he had done that, but Parker had only half listened to him so he couldn't remember the reason. "He needed extra help, I understand." It was a guess.

"General Williams has been on the base."

That hit a nerve. Parker's face flushed. "You have destroyed that man, forced him out of the service over the loss of a single plane. Can't you just leave him alone?"

The senator cleared his throat. "You don't see what's going on right under your nose, do you? They found something. They have taken one of the hard drives out of the archive and they're running models with it. They are trying to figure out where that plane is. I want you to know that the plane is the property of the United States and if anything happens to it, I will hold you personally responsible." Senator James turned on his heels and stomped out of the office.

A lot of the senator's threats were just hot air, but if the man wanted to, he could make someone's life miserable, as he had to General Williams. Parker took the threat seriously.

Getting up from his chair, he walked out to his aide and said, "Get me a car. I need to pay Colonel Ross a visit."

"Yes, Sir."

General Parker barged into the conference room Ross was using as a headquarters without bothering to knock. Both the major and colonel looked up with surprise. "What's going on here?" Parker looked over at Dempsey's computer screen. "Have you found the plane?"

"No, Sir," Ross was quick to say.

"What's on the screen, then? Why are you running scenarios on the ocean bed?"

"Just exploring possibilities." Dempsey thought about turning off his computer, but decided that would be too obvious.

"I want this program shut down by tomorrow, do you understand? All of this equipment needs to be gone and the final report on my desk. I'll have your new orders in the morning. I don't want Senator James snooping around ever again. That's an order." Parker turned and walked out.

"The game is up," Ross said.

"What are the chances we will end up anywhere near each other when we get our orders?" Dempsey said.

"Slim and none. Are you done with the last model yet?"

"Yes, Sir. I just finished it."

"It will have to do. I just hope that Williams was able to get a boat and some equipment. We will have to do it this weekend. We won't know where we're going to be after that."

Dempsey printed out the report and then erased the file. After shutting down the computer, he opened up the case and pulled out the hard drive. "What do you want me to do with this?"

Ross thought for a second and then said, "Bring it with us. It will get dropped in the bottom of the ocean. I will put a blank hard drive into the archives. They will think that they have the real one, but I doubt they'd check it."

"Sounds like a plan. I guess we will be meeting clandestinely over the next few days."

"I'll pay the general a visit. I don't trust the phones. We need to move up our timeline. Senator James is breathing down our necks."

Ross shut down his computer and pulled out the report that he had written a few weeks ago. It omitted anything to do with Dalton's information that had been found underneath the chimney at General Williams' house. It was something Ross wanted to keep quiet.

Chapter Fifty

The boat chugged up and back, with three fishing lines in the water. There were no hooks, just weights to make it look like they were on a fishing charter. There was a large cable with electrical line out the back of the ship, for the side scanning radar. Other than that, the disguise was perfect.

A captain and three crew members were on the boat. Two of the men were in the cabin, monitoring the images of the sea floor. The other was watching to make sure the cables weren't getting tangled. The captain spent most of his time in the flying bridge, steering the ship, but came down once in a while to check the status of the operation.

They'd been doing this for four days now. They had covered all the places that the plane should have come down. Dempsey brought out his laptop again. He was losing faith in his estimates. He had gone over and over the model. The plane had to be here. Right here.

He heard the radio call up to the captain. "Sir, we have the object again, but there's nothing else here."

The captain throttled back on the engines. "Get a fix on it. At least we can dive on that. Maybe it's a piece of it, anyway."

"Yes, Sir."

The boat stopped and the anchor dropped. The captain came down the ladder. "We don't have anything but that one object we keep coming across. I'm sending my men down to take pictures of it. It might be a clue as to what's going on."

A crewmember poked his head out of the hatch. "Sir, that ship that's been shadowing us is approaching fast."

"Start reeling in, gentlemen. Make it look like you have a fish on, if possible," the captain replied.

The ship was quickly in view, bearing down on them.

"Coast Guard. Maybe they think we're smuggling drugs. If they search the ship, they are going to be very curious as to what we're doing," Ross said. His shoulders sagged.

A crewmember on the Coast Guard cutter put a bullhorn up to his mouth. "This is the United States Coast Guard. Prepare to be boarded."

"Looks like we have company," the captain said with a sigh.

The cutter threw lines over and soon the two ships were tied up to each other. Five sailors with full combat gear and guns were soon aboard. The cutter's captain joined them.

"Colonel Ross, General Anderson, and Major Dempsey, I have warrants for your arrest."

Dempsey looked over to the other two. *How do they know our names?*

"On what charges?" Anderson bellowed.

"Destruction of government property, theft of government property, dereliction of duty and whatever else Senator

James can think up." He motioned to two of his men. Soon Dempsey, Williams, and Ross were all sitting on the deck of the Coast Guard ship. All the equipment from the boat was brought over and several of the sailors had donned suits and were diving down onto the object.

"They've been watching us the whole time," Dempsey muttered.

"Yes, and we led them right to what they wanted us to," Ross said.

"How's this all going to end?" Dempsey looked around. The crew members from the boat were brought over, and after the divers returned, the small boat was taken under tow.

"This is the end of the line," Ross replied.

Williams leaned against the bulkhead and closed his eyes.

Dempsey shifted in his seat and watched the land get closer and closer. "I hope they don't find it. They'll use it again and destroy time."

"If the thing was there, we would have found it," Ross said.

"I could be wrong in my model. The ship's logs could have given the wrong latitude and longitude. The plane could be beyond repair. There are endless possibilities."

"Or, someone could have beaten us to the thing. It's been down there a long time."

"None of the charges will stick, especially the dereliction of duty. None of us were on duty at the time," Anderson said, his eyes still closed.

On shore, they were all put in the brig then they were being brought out one at a time for questioning. Dempsey was the last to be escorted into the interview room. An Air Force MP stood guard while General Parker and Senator James sat across from the Major.

"Was this all some type of joke?" Senator James' beady eyes tried to bore holes through him, it seemed.

"I don't know what you mean, Sir."

"You've destroyed information, wiped hard drives and now you sent us on a wild goose chase. What are you trying to hide?" James' face was red.

"We were just out hanging around, fishing, Sir."

"With side-scanning sonar and enough sophisticated equipment to make an admiral jealous? I don't think so. What were you looking for? Before you answer that, I want you to know we've already run the model you had on your laptop, so we know you were looking for something."

Dempsey swallowed hard. He didn't know what the others had told them, and he didn't know what was down there. He debated about giving them what they wanted, but he looked the senator in the eyes and remembered how much he hated the man. "We found what we were looking for. That small object we were about to dive on. That was what we were looking for."

The senator sat back in his seat. Dempsey looked at the general. *What's that look?* He wondered. *Is it sympathy?*"

"Take him back to his cell."

"You have the same answer from all three of them. They were looking for the marker. You have no reason to hold them. I am ordering their release." The general said.

"You can't do that. They know where the airplane is. We need to hold them until they confess."

The general was undaunted. He stood up and said, "Good day, Senator."

An hour later all three of the prisoners had been brought into a conference room, their handcuffs removed. A minute later, General Parker came in. He laid a stack of pictures on the desk. "I don't know if you already know what the marker said, but if you didn't, I brought you pictures of it. All of the made up charges have been dropped. As for Major Dempsey and Colonel Ross, you are to report to me on next Monday where you'll be reassigned. General Williams, you have a good day." He turned to leave then stopped and faced them one more time. "Gentlemen, you have my sympathies."

Ross looked at the photo. It showed a granite large cross with the inscription, 'Captain Gerald Myers. Born September 15, 2012. Died January 6, 1894.'

Sample Chapter

Millennium Man

Chapter 1: Montana

Two Marines stood guard at the door. Director Phillip James walked to the most secure part of the top secret facility. It was deep in the mountains of Montana. Unlike NORAD, that had all sorts of publicity in comparison, this was a small operation. It was built with one single purpose, to support the Millennium Man. The hallway looked just like any hospital hallway in America, clean and white with the slight smell of antiseptic cleaners.

Six foot two, with short brown hair, Phil was slender, a man that most women would consider attractive. Phil walked up to the guards at the door. He was in his white lab coat and carried a clip board. There was so much computer data being used your street clothes had to be covered up at all times by a lab coat. All dust and dirt was to be kept at a minimum both for the health of the man they guarded and the highly sensitive electrical equipment in the complex. The clip board did not have charts and graphs on it like most clip boards of executives. Phil had a bad memory and always carried the clip board to write notes and reminders on.

The building had white cinderblock walls. Drop down florescent lights illuminated the halls and rooms. Every part of the building was cleaned regularly to keep dust at a minimum. Everyone who worked there also lived there, to limit the flow of information that left the complex. Phillip had just left his office and made his way down to where the Millennium Man lived. He had been ill of late and Phil was going to check up on him. It was the only reason he would venture to this part of the building. Otherwise he would gladly stay away.

The Marine guard scanned Phil's badge, although he recognized him. When the machine dinged, the guard nodded his approval and then opened the door for Phil.

The room he entered into was brightly lit and full of medical equipment. Two doctors, five nurses and many medical assistants all stood around the bed of the patient. They had been trying to revive him for two hours. By the time Phil had arrived, they had given up.

The doctor turned to face Phil and just shook his head. "It's over. There is nothing else we can do."

"It can't be over; in this time of terror threats, we need him more than ever," Phil protested.

"He's dead." The doctor walked out of the room followed by most of the nurses and medical assistants.

The other doctor stayed. "Write *this* on your clipboard. Time of death, January 16th at 7:50 pm," he said. He was Rick Allred, the best of the best when it came to medical doctors. Paying his huge salary was not a problem with the United States Government bankrolling the project. He had black hair and stood a couple of inches shorter than Phil. He was getting a slight pot belly, but at fifty-two, he didn't care. He had no family close to him after his last divorce. He had no intention of starting over with another romance.

"What are we going to do?"

"Find the next one. "

Phil didn't know what that meant. He had been hired after the Millennium Man was already here. "How do we do that?"

"Quickly. The Blues are playing god with us. They only make one Millennium Man at a time. Whoever it is, we have to find him and get him here before his powers fully develop."

It was an alien race that they called the Blues. Even though their ships were undetectable by normal radar, the United States had developed a type of pulse radar that picked them up. The blips on the radar turned blue when it detected one of the alien ships. The name had stuck. They had no idea who the Blues were, only that they had the power to turn the human brain into something with telepathic abilities. This greatly enhanced the fight against terror, having someone who could find threats from afar.

The only problem is the Blues only did it to one person at a time, so the agency would find and kidnap that person. They had tried to mimic the alien technology a few times, but it only resulted in the death of the person they transplanted it into. The interface was so intermingled with the brain that massive brain swelling always resulted and death followed shortly after. The aliens had gotten around this somehow.

"What if they don't make another one in the United States?" Phil wanted answers. He was supposed to be the Director of the operation, but he still had a lot to learn. The loss of the Millennium Man had come too soon.

"Let's see, a man that can read everyone else's mind, even from great distances suddenly appeared in the midst of an enemy regime? They would know all of our secrets and every move we were going to make before we made it. It would be a catastrophe. The very thought makes me shudder. We had better hope that they don't do that. They have always made them here in the North America. We had one from Canada once. Kidnapping him in a foreign country and sneaking him across the border was a feat, let me tell you. Hopefully the aliens will pick a younger man this time. We seem to only get twenty years out of the Millennium Men we get, almost to the day."

"I wasn't here when we found the last one. I don't know how to go about it," Phil admitted.

"Any weird newspaper headlines about abductions or UFOs in the sky have to be followed up on in great detail. We have to capture the new Millennium Man before he figures out how to use the new power he is given. Otherwise he will know you are coming and you will never catch up with him."

"When should I start looking?" Phil asked.

Dr. Allred looked down at his watch. "Now. As a matter of fact, I would not be going to bed tonight, if I were you."

Phil got out his clipboard and jotted down a note about looking for UFOs and reported abductions. He then rushed up to his office and turned on his computer and started scanning the internet.

Dr. Allred also went to his office, but instead of scanning the internet he got on the phone and called his friend in the Air Force, General Morgan. "Hi, Fred, you know those blue radar blips that you are not supposed to talk about?"

"Yes?"

"I need you to track them and send me locations for any of them that stopped for more than ten minutes."

There was silence over the phone for a few seconds and then the General said, "He's dead, then?" It wasn't the sound of sadness in his voice, but more of an annoyed sound.

"Yes, he's gone."

"I will send you the data."

Made in the USA
San Bernardino, CA
15 August 2016